T0196343

IN THE CITY OF SHADOWS

DAKOTA KIRKPATRICK

authorHOUSE®

AuthorHouse™
1663 Liberty Drive
Bloomington, IN 47403
www.authorhouse.com
Phone: 1 (800) 839-8640

Published by AuthorHouse   06/15/2017

ISBN: 978-1-5246-9681-8 (sc)
ISBN: 978-1-5246-9679-5 (hc)
ISBN: 978-1-5246-9680-1 (e)

Library of Congress Control Number: 2017909382

Print information available on the last page.

Any people depicted in stock imagery provided by Thinkstock are models,
and such images are being used for illustrative purposes only.
Certain stock imagery © Thinkstock.

This book is printed on acid-free paper.

Contents

The Hollows

Minutes pass, seconds taking an eternity as I stare at the clock on the wall. Time ticking life away as I just sit here staring, waiting, ready for it to strike eight o'clock so I can finally leave this place. I'm sitting in an old metal fold up chair at a tiny junk covered desk, deep underground, working the graveyard shift at the local subway station. I am the supervisor of the so called "security services" down here.

Don't have a clue what I am actually securing beyond a meal for the rats scurrying around when I drop dead from boredom. Day in and day out I sit here staring at the clock, nothing ever happens, no one ever comes, no one ever goes. The silence is enough to make you crazy, I am not even allowed a radio to listen to. They say it will distract me from any security threats, yeah, right.

Even if there were an actual risk to any security here, I would be less than useless, I don't carry any weapon, no pepper spray, not even handcuffs. I have no authority to even tell someone to stop what they are doing, it's a joke. Say someone here was being held at gunpoint, all I could do is be like, oh no, don't worry, you only have to wait to be saved till I can find a phone and call the cops, then wait till they get here, I'm sure the psycho with the gun will be very understanding and wait too.

I'm stuck in a little corner room just off to the side of the subway tracks, the walls are all concrete and blank, just a single circle clock on them. Just about five more minutes. The room begins shaking violently as the morning subway flies through the tunnels to a halt at the station dock. Hundreds of people quickly walk out of the subway, most in formal attire, on their way to work. A few vagrants also stumble out, looking for a place around the station to call home.

The entire world seems to pass by, not noticing me, not caring about anything, not that I really care, it would just be nice to be more than the nothing I am here.

The clock strikes eight, the small watch on my wrist beeps at me, letting me know I can reclaim my freedom again. The door to the small room flies open as Jim, the next shift guard walks in. He's wearing our standard uniform, grey button up shirt with black dress pants, his shirt loosely tucked in his pants. A small sewn on badge stating security is on the left pocket of the shirt. A meaningless patch for a meaningless position, fitting.

The guy is ancient, at least eighty years old, he looks similar to a mad scientist, his white hair only around the sides of his head and shooting out like he was electrocuted. Wrinkles cover his body making his face droop. He's a real asshole to top it off, that is if he speaks to you at all. He typically ignores anything you say, but whatever he's here, now I can go.

"Have fun." I say, waving at Jim as I walk out the door.

He doesn't answer, he just waves me out.

I make my way around the station to the stairs that lead to the outside world. Graffiti covers most of the walls, can't really make out what any of them say though. As I go up the stairs, the light from the sun blasts down, blinding me. There is a chill as the wind blows through the stair well. The smell of car fumes and pollution fill the city, thank God, I don't live here.

I live just outside the city in a little farm town suburb, the place is so small if you asked anyone from the city, they wouldn't even know where you were talking about. I like it that way though, it's quiet, peaceful, secluded.

My car is parked just outside the station, the one perk of the place is that I don't have to pay a stupid meter to park here. My car has definitely seen better days, my bumper is hanging off, and the side mirrors are nonexistent. All the paint is rusted and chipped away, I've had the thing for at least fifteen years. It was my first car, got it when I turned sixteen, I'm just amazed it still runs.

I hop in my car, it takes a few tries before the engine roars to life, gears grinding, like the car has given up on life. I adjust the rear-view mirror, glancing back at all the cars flying back and forth. I let out a sigh, then start driving towards home.

2

feel my life is stuck in a pitiful circle, everything always stays the same day after day, even the route I take to and from work is the same. Never taking the road off the beaten track. The city is now in my rear view as I pull onto the highway. Nothing but corn fields and emptiness lie ahead.

It takes about forty-five minutes to make it home. The bumps in the road from years of neglect bounce and shake the car as I go. I pass a few old abandoned farm houses and weather torn barns, before the city was built this whole area was once a thriving town for farmers and country folk, now they have all been pushed away and most of their land was stolen by the city people with deep pockets.

I pass by several old gravel roads zig zagging this way and that, all leading to the town that once was. I come up to an old dirt road I used to take to and from work before the city closed it off due to suspicious activity that was reported, it cuts my drive in half, never understood why they closed it, there was never an official reasoning behind it. They just put up a road closed sign one day and that was that.

"Screw it." I said.

I whip my car around and head down the old closed road, going around the small road closed sign. I figure I know this is the fastest way home and I need a change in my boring, empty routine.

The dirt is dried and solid, making the ride fairly smooth. Small dirt and rock mounds make cliff like overhangs along the sides of the road. Hundreds of dying trees line the shoulders, giving the appearance of a forest. I roll my window down, breathing in the crisp spring air. There is a bit of a chill, but it's worth it, even this slightest difference in my day is refreshing.

A dense layer of fog is filling the road just ahead where the trees prevent the sun from entering. The fog is so thick you can only see a few feet ahead. My car begins to sputter out a grinding sound, it begins to stall and slow. It jerks with every foot I drive; the engine gives out and my car comes to a halt. The dense fog is surrounding me now.

"Damn it, you piece of crap." I yell.

I smack the steering wheel, and crank the key, trying to get the engine to turn over. The car just makes a grinding sound as the engine cries, trying to start. I stop and wait a few seconds, looking out at the fog. I must be only about ten minutes from home.

Of course, this would be my luck for trying to make my tedious day any better. I sit in silence for a few minutes, just to give the car a short break. Then the radio shoots out so loud my eardrums feel they will burst, and an eerie song begins playing with the sound of children chanting some kids' song. They sing something about, "it's only just begun."

My heart is racing, I turn the radio off, then frantically start turning the key again. The engine screeches, trying to turn over, smoke sputters out of my exhaust as the car roars to life. I shift into drive and look up at the road ahead. A woman is standing in the fog about twenty feet ahead.

Her head is tilted down, like she's looking at the ground. She's wearing a ripped up white dress with dirt smeared up from the bottom. She is engulfed in the fog, her long black hair covering her face. She appears to have a collection of bruise marks up and down her arms, they are a dark red, almost black. Her skin is pale as snow.

She isn't moving, not even an inch, as if she's not even breathing. I rub my hands on my eyes, thinking maybe I'm imagining things. There's no way someone would be out on this road, especially walking around.

I begin driving slowly forward, only one to two miles per hour, trying not to spook the young woman. I want to ask if she needs help, but something feels wrong, I fear the thought of even speaking to her.

The closer I get to her, the farther away she seems to be, as if I'm reversing away, rather than moving forward. I glance down at my gear shift, confused, it says I'm still in drive. I look back up and she's gone, vanished into the fog. I feel a twinge in my spine, an unsettling feeling builds in the pit of my stomach. I begin driving faster, keeping my head on a swivel to make sure I don't accidentally run into her.

I go for miles, never catching a glimpse of the young woman, or any vehicle she may have been in, just nothingness. I drive on and the fog begins lifting, letting the sun retake the earth. I turn off the old dirt road onto a small highway to the left. My house is just up over the next couple hills.

As I pull up to the house I see my daughter, Eve, outside swinging on the old tire swing attached to the large oak tree in the front yard. She looks just like her mother, beyond her strange taste in clothing. She has a long colorful dress on, with paint splattered legging type of pants. My son, Danny, is playing with a toy gun nearby, shooting invisible targets. He is dressed up like a soldier, wearing all camo. I park the car and hop out, still trying to shake the strange feeling in my stomach.

"Daddy." Eve says, as she runs up and gives me a hug.

"Hey, sweetie, how was your day?" I ask, crouching down to her level.

"Boring, we didn't get to go to the park today, mommy said she was too busy. So, I was stuck here with him all day." She said, pointing at her brother.

Danny sticks out his tongue at her, then goes back to playing.

"Well, maybe you can go tomorrow." I say. She shrugs her shoulders and runs back over to the swing. I stand up and look at the house. It's in pretty rough shape, the white paint that once covered it is chipped away, and turned a dingy shade. The roof has chunks of shingles missing all over it, several of the rain gutters have fallen off. The window to the attic is cracked from the big hail storm last summer. The small cement steps to the front door have eroded, and cracked, as well as gained a slant from the dirt below settling.

I walk into the house, my wife, Margaret, is standing I the kitchen washing dishes. We have to do them by hand ever since our dishwasher broke, not that that thing ever got the dishes clean anyway, but it gave the illusion of simplicity. She always dresses like she has to impress someone, even in the house. She has a fancy looking black dress on, with the tall heeled shoes to top it off. Her hair she doesn't mess with much, her bright blonde hair pulled back in a ponytail. She looks sort of like she's going to a funeral, but also with the slight look of a librarian, strange combination, but it works.

"I'm home." I state, throwing my uniform top onto an old half broken coat rack by the door.

Margaret turns and smiles at me. "Wow, you got home early today." She said, still washing the plate in her hand.

"Yeah, I took the old dirt road that the city closed."

"Oh? Is that safe to take?" She asked, looking concerned.

I shrug. "Seemed safe enough to me, the old junker out there broke down on me though. Oh, and there was some woman out there walking around, I think she was lost or something."

She pulls the plug on the sink letting the water go down the drain, then dries off her hands. She puts her hands on her hips. "A woman? Did you help her?" She asked, giving me a crooked look.

"Well, I might have but she didn't exactly stick around for me to try." I say, glancing down at the spaces between the wooden floor boards.

"Huh, well I hope she's alright." She said, walking out of the kitchen. "You want to do anything today?" She shouts back to me.

"I don't know, do you?" I ask.

"Well, I would like to go into the city real fast, I need a few groceries from the store." She said.

"Okay, just let me take a shower and get a few things done and we will head out." I say. God, back to the city I guess, don't know why she couldn't have given me a heads up, I could have stopped earlier.

"Great, I'll go get ready." She says, as she walks up the stairs to the bedroom.

Get ready? How much readier can you be, already looking like that.

I shrug it off, and head up the stairs to the bathroom, turning on the shower water to let it heat up. The place is so old and broken it takes an hour for the water heater to kick in. Even then you only get a few minutes of actual warm water before it freezes you again.

3

glance up at the small digital clock on the shelf above the fireplace. It's already seven o'clock at night. Margaret is still not ready yet, a bit ridiculous at this point, should've taken a nap. At least tomorrow is my day off, but still.

Ten more minutes' pass before Margaret finally comes down the stairs, she looks exactly the same as before, just more crap on her face. I never understood the point of makeup, in my opinion it makes you look worse not better.

"I'm ready." She says.

I let out a sigh. "Alright, let's go. Danny, Eve, we're leaving, let's go." I say.

The kids come out of their rooms and head to the car, I wait at the door already knowing that Margaret will actually have ten more things to do before she actually leaves.

Right on cue as Margaret heads to the door, she stops.

"One sec, I gotta pee." She says, walking to the bathroom.

A few minutes later she returns. The kids begin honking the horn out in the car to speed her up.

"Oh, hold on, forgot my purse." She says, walking over to the small table in the dining room.

It's like clockwork every time. She finally makes it out the door and hops into the car. I lock the front door, then get in the car myself. The sun has already set at this point, light glints off the windows from the moon.

I start up the car and back out of the driveway and we head off down the road. We go over a couple hills, and I take the short cut down the dirt road again. I want to get this trip over as fast as possible.

The fog is still thick in the air, drifting lazily across the road. It is already pitch black out here even with my high beams on. The same eerie feeling creeps up on me again as it did this morning. The small cliffs along the shoulder are barely visible. The dead trees along the road seem to warn you away, like the small forest of trees are hiding something.

The fog is so dense I must slow the car down just to keep on the road. I feel the hairs on my neck stand up, sending a chill down my spine. I don't know what it is about this fog that gets to me. Maybe just the environment itself, maybe just that I can't see what may or may not be out there.

"Honey? Are we almost out of here? This place gives me the creeps." Margaret said, glancing quickly out the windows.

I forget how to speak for a moment, tripping over words in my throat. "It can't be much further." I say.

I look around at the small cliffs again, they look the same as the ones I was just looking at, almost as if we're not even moving or we are stuck in a loop of some sort.

"Look daddy! There's someone over there." Eve shouts, pointing at the trees to the left of us.

I look over at the trees, but nothing appears to be there. Must be some childhood imagination or something. Then again, I did see that woman out here earlier. I shake my head, trying to forget about it and just focus on getting out of here.

After being in this fog for so long, I get why they closed this road. It's enough to make you crazy.

"Daddy, there they are again." Eve says, still pointing at the trees.

"Honey, there is no one..." I stop, catching sight of several small children scattered between the trees just beyond the road. They are all pale white, like corpses in a morgue, boys and girls, ranging from toddlers to teenagers. A tingle shoots down my spine as my heart begins to pound. I freeze, words escaping me, as if the children's gaze has stolen my voice.

They are all staring directly at us, black circles surround their eyes. I feel a cold sweat sweep over me. Margaret is stunned her mouth wide open, frozen in fear. She tries to mouth out a few words, but they never come.

I look back to where the children were, but they have disappeared, vanished into the fog and trees. The car begins to jerk and sputter just as it had earlier.

"No, no, no, no, no." I repeat, stomping my foot down on the gas pedal, praying the car will keep pushing forward.

"What's going on?" Margaret asks, her hands bracing onto the door and dashboard.

"I don't know, somethings wrong." I reply, trying to jerk the car forward with my bodyweight.

The kids hold onto each other in the backseat, making whimpering noises. The car makes a grinding sound, then a loud snapping sound, like metal collapsing into itself. The car slows to a halt, angled towards the trees on the right.

My heart is pounding now, my hands begin to shake. I look out around us, nothing but thick fog surrounds. I try turning the key, nothing, not the slightest sound, the car has given up entirely.

"Shit!" I shout, slamming my hand on the steering wheel. "Margaret, is there anything in the glovebox? Flashlight, tools, something?"

She opens the glovebox, rummaging through a pile of old papers that have been left and forgotten over the years. She pulls out a small screwdriver and an old headlamp.

"This is all I could find." She states, handing them to me.

The screwdriver will be useless, I'm no mechanic, even if I had any real tools, I would never be able to fix anything. I put the headlamp on, it flickers a bit, then glows a dim light. The batteries are probably half dead.

I hop out of the car. "Stay put, I'll be right back." I pop the hood, looking to see what could be wrong. Everything looks like it should be working, I shut the hood then lie down on the ground, shining what little light I have underneath the car. There is a metal bar or pipe hanging down from the car, no doubt whatever is wrong with it. I reach in and grab onto the pipe, trying to yank it free, but it doesn't budge.

"Damn it, can't I just catch a break, just once?" I whisper to myself.

I slide out from under the car and hop up. I shine the light around the road and into the trees. I have a strange feeling building up in my stomach, I can't see anything. The air is cold, far colder than it should be. It was eighty degrees all day long, but my breath comes out in small shuddered clouds in front of me.

I hop back in the car. "The car is done for, there is some kind of metal pipe or something busted under the damn thing." I say, letting out a sigh.

"Are you serious?" Margaret pleads, a concerned look on her face.

The kids are still huddled together in the back, they seem terrified, their eyes squeezed shut, letting out small squeaks of panic.

I grab my phone from my front pocket, no service, of course.

"Honey, does your phone have any signal here?" I ask.

She digs through her purse, searching for her phone through piles of trash she left in the things. Might as well be carrying a fancy garbage bag with her everywhere.

She finally pulls out her phone, pressing a few buttons on it. "It's dead, I forgot to charge it today. Sorry." She said, giving me a guilty look.

I shake my head at her. Of course you did, you can't manage to do anything can you. It's always nice to know you can't count on your partner when you need them.

I look out at the small cliffs just beyond the shoulder. I bet I can get at least one bar up there, enough to make a call to someone.

"I'm going to try to get up to those…" I begin, as the radio shoots to life, blaring that same song with the children chanting, "it's only just begun."

Eve and Danny begin screaming from the backseat, my heart is pounding out of my chest. I try to turn off the radio but it won't stop or turn down. I grab the screwdriver and repeatedly stab it into the radio, trying to get it to break and shut off. The radio wiggles loose from its home in my dash, I grab the whole thing and rip it out, wires break and set it free. I toss the radio out onto the dirt road, but the music doesn't stop.

"I have to get up on that cliff, maybe I can get a signal, get someone, anyone out here to help us." I state, grabbing Margaret's arm.

She shakes her head at me. "No, don't go out there." She begs, tears forming in her eyes.

"It's the only way, we can't just wait here." I say.

"I will be right back, if I run it will only take a few minutes." I state.

Margaret pulls me in to her, giving me a quick, scared kiss. "You come back to us, you hear me?" She pleads.

I jump out of the car and begin sprinting into the dead trees, the cliff is only a few yards away. The dim light of the headlamp shines just enough to see my footing. So far, so good.

My heart is pounding and my lungs exploding from the run, I really am in no shape for running. I haven't run in years, but the fear building deep in my gut is willing me forward.

The headlamp illuminates small items littered across the ground. I pass by trash and broken bottles. Small broken toys are strung out along the dead grass, as if someone was playing with them out here. They are not simply thrown here, they are set up, like a crime scene reenactment.

I stop and look closer at the arrangement of toys, a panic shoots right through me. The toys are set up with a toy car angled to the right, with four dolls, two lying beside the car, one off to the side near some twigs set up like a forest, and one down the road.

These toys are set up to recreate us, like this was someone's sick plan, I have to hurry. I begin sprinting towards the cliff once again, closing in on it, I run through the thick tall grass that covers it. I finally make it to its peak, holding my cell phone up as high as I can, begging for just one bar, just the smallest signal.

4

Nothing, not even a trace of a signal, I have 911 pre-dialed into the phone ready to hit the call button. I jump into the air, hoping it will get those extra inches to a signal.

The phone flashes a small signal as I jump. "Yes!" I hit the send button and jump up and down repeatedly. The call finally goes through.

"911 emergen…how may.. help…" The dispatcher cuts in and out.

"Help! We are stranded, send help." I shout at the phone.

The call ends as the phone loses the signal again. I hope that was enough to get someone out here. I look down at the car, I can just make out someone moving around outside the car.

"Damn it, what are they doing?" I mumble.

I begin heading back towards the car, running as fast as my legs allow. The scream of a woman screeches through the air, and a shiver goes down my spine, I begin sprinting towards the sound. Another shriek flies through the air, I pass by the set-up toys again, only now the dolls have been rearranged, no time to stop and look.

I run between the line on dead trees, nearly tripping over the garbage thrown in the grass. I look around at the dirt road but nothing is there, I run over to the car and hop inside.

"Is everyone okay?" I ask, looking around the car making sure everyone is accounted for.

They all give me a scared nod, all fearing to make any sounds. The radio outside has fallen silent now. No sign of movement outside.

"Were any of you out of the car a minute ago?" I ask, darting glances to each of them.

"No, we haven't moved an inch." Margaret responds. "Did you get help?"

"I don't know, I got a call out to the police, but I'm not sure they could hear me." I say, looking out into the thick fog.

Minutes feel like hours as we sit in silence, praying the police arrive. I stare out into the fog, watching for any form of movement.

"Dad… What is that over there?" Danny questions, looking into the trees.

Small glowing green dots, like eyes, line the trees. They look as though a thousand cat eyes are staring out at us.

"I don't know Danny, just don't look at them." I respond.

I don't know anything anymore. The radio outside in the dirt begins to make a scratching sound of static. Then that ear-piercing song begins to play again.

I close my eyes trying to ignore it, to wake up from this terrible dream. Such relief never comes. I open my eyes, looking back over towards the radio as it sings its song. Off in the trees behind the radio those small children have reappeared, but they aren't looking at us, instead they are looking down the road ahead, pointing.

I turn my head slowly to see what they are pointing to, dreading what I may find. Down the road standing, shrouded in the fog is that woman I seen earlier. Her head tilted downward just as before. She has a ghostly presence, almost like she is the fog itself, transparent. She stands there, still and silent.

My lungs breathe out air in stuttered breaths, the icy air feels like it's choking me. I can't move, can't take my eyes off her, afraid what she may do.

"Roy? Who is that?" Margaret asks me, her body quivering in her seat.

I can't speak, as if the woman has a hold on me, stealing my words before I can make them. As if I'm paralyzed. Then a loud smack hits the car windows at all sides. I fly backwards, straight out of my skin, the small children are completely surrounding the vehicle, pounding on the windows. They are now chanting the same song as the radio, as they pound on the car.

Danny and Eve are screaming, crowding onto the backseat floor boards, Margaret shrieks and covers her head with her arms. The terror that has struck me is more than I can explain, I stare out at the children as the bang into the car, their faces are that of something you would see in a movie. Something unnatural, ghostly and dead. My heart is ripping out of my chest, I can no longer breathe, I am in complete shock. My entire world feels silent, like I've gone deaf.

I squeeze my eyes shut so tight, they feel as though they may tear straight out of my eyelids. Then nothing, everything faded to black, emptiness.

5

I'm not sure if I'm dreaming or awake. I'm no longer in a car, and I'm alone. I look around, I'm still on the old dirt road. It seems different, the sun is shining down, the fog is gone, the grass and trees are full of life. Green and yellow leaves fill the trees. You can hear the birds singing as they fly through the skies.

I begin walking down the dirt road, feeling the warmth shining down. The small cliffs behind the trees tower over the road. This is the road I remember, way back before it was ever closed. I used to drive this every day, it was beautiful. The fog was hiding every ounce of peace this road once held.

I continue walking, taking in the crisp spring air, feeling the calm. This must be a dream, I don't understand. I gaze out trying to find an answer to why I have ended up here, I see nothing.

The trees branch out as if they are trying to swallow the road. I look out at the next cliffs, it's taller than the last, with a tall dead oak tree on top of it. Something is moving up there, I squint my eyes trying to make out the moving figures. I start running, trying to get close enough to see what is up there.

Then I see it, the woman from the fog, she is up on the cliff kneeling in the grass. She looks as though she is praying, but she is not alone. There is a group of men standing behind her, one has a pitchfork aimed at the back of her head, as the others hook something up to the tree.

I sneak closer, crouching so I'm not noticed. I'm just below, crouching near the tree lines of the road. The woman has her eyes closed, the men are shouting something at her, I can't make out the words. The men then grab her and lift her up, as she mouths out a few words. They put a rope around her neck, she then opens her eyes, staring straight at me. I feel her eyes hit me like a hammer to the chest.

Then men then pull the rope, it slides through the top of the tree as the woman's feet come off the ground. They lift her high up, overlooking the road, they tie the end of the rope to the tree. The woman shakes and writhes in the air, clinging to her last breaths. The men stand and watch as the life slips from her, they laugh and yell holding their pitchforks high.

They turn and head down the hill of the cliff, fading into the distance. I stay there watching the woman, her eyes still wide open aiming right at me. Her mouth opens wide and a shriek shoots from it, making my ears bleed. I squeeze my eyes shut from the pain.

I opened my eyes, I'm back in the car, but the shrieking is real, the woman is in front of the car. Her ghostly mouth is wide open enough to swallow the car whole, sending her screams right through me. I cover my ears, eyes wide. She is holding something in her hands.

A noose. The doors fly off the car, ripping straight from their hinges. Margaret is yanked out of the front, the ghostly children surround her chanting, "you're our mother now," they drag her off into the tree line as she screams.

"Margaret!" I scream, trying to reach out to her.

I feel a sharp push on my chest, sending me flying out of the car. I land face first in the dirt, getting a mouth full of the bitter, grisly earth. I spit the muck out and turn to see the woman grabbing Eve and Danny from the car.

I push off the ground back to my feet, sprinting over to them.

"Danny, Eve, run!" I scream.

Another blast hits me in the chest shooting me back, smashing into the trees. I fall into the tall dead grass, my head pounding from the concussion, my brain feels scrambled. I lift my head up with every ounce of strength I have left, all my air has left my lungs.

I look up to see the woman, she has Eve by the arm yanking her out of the car. I try to crawl over to them, my arms weak. Danny is in her other arm now, she pulls them out onto the ground. I can barely see, all lights in my head are turning off, I can't help but give in. Then nothing.

6

I open my eyes, disoriented, I look around trying to focus. Everything is blurry, my head pounding behind my eyes. I can't move my arms, as if they are bound behind my back. I can make out the grass around me, I'm not on the road. Where am I, my focus slowly comes back, I can hear something being pulled behind me.

I look around, squinting my eyes. I'm on the cliff, I can see the road below, all the small ghostly children are standing by the car. Margaret is standing there with them, she looks pale just like them, they are all staring up at me. Watching, like they are waiting for someone to address them.

A small hand touches my shoulder, I look to see Eve and Danny standing one on each side of me. They are smiling at me.

"Eve, Danny, thank God, are you okay?" I ask, letting out a sigh of relief.

They don't speak, just keep smiling at me. Then a rope goes over my head, tightening around my neck. A rise in panic builds inside me, this is where she was hung. The ghostly woman walks in from of me, giving me a once over, then a twisted smirk grows across her face.

The woman let's out a paralyzing few words, "it's your turn now."

"No, you can't do this, it wasn't my fault they did that to you." I frantically look at my children. "Eve, Danny, get this thing off me. You have to help me."

"It's okay daddy, it's better this way." Eve says, a cold crooked smile on her face.

"Yes, better." Danny agrees.

"What the fuck's wrong with you, this isn't better. I am your father, stop this." I plead.

The rope gets tighter around my throat, pulling me up to my feet.

"Help! Help!" I scream, as I shake my body around trying to break free.

The rope lifts me up off my feet, squirming in the air. My body writhing, shaking, begging for life.

"Help, me." I squeak out.

Eve, and Danny stare up at me, holding the ghostly woman's hands.

"Goodbye, daddy." Eve and Danny say, waving at me as the walk off with the woman.

I can't breathe, the pressure around my throat choking me. The world begins to dim, as the fog closes in on me, swallowing me, into nothing.

The 8th Floor

I cocked my gun back, chambering a round. This is the closest thing to real action I've seen in the last eight years. I am a private investigator, hired to follow a young man around by his wife, who assumes he is being unfaithful to her. He goes by the name Thomas Duncan. I had satisfied Mrs. Duncan's questions on the matter about fifteen minutes ago, needless to say she didn't take the news well.

I had followed the man into several hotels throughout this week, as he entertained ladies of the night so to speak. I snapped a few pictures and brought them to Mrs. Duncan. I tend to stick around after the job is done, making sure when the other party is confronted things don't get too out of hand.

That was not the case here, things had quickly taken a turn. I watched from my car to see how things would play out. Shortly after Mr. Duncan arrived at their home the screaming began, only a few minutes had passed before the house fell silent. Then came the gunshots, at least three rounds were fired in the house before I knew I had to intervene.

I ran up to the front door, staying to the side, so not to catch a stray bullet myself. I tried to peek in through the window, but they had their blinds drawn.

"Mrs. Duncan? Is everything okay?" I ask, through the door.

No answer. I slowly pulled the door open and peeked in, blood was splattered across the fresh white carpet. I slid in quietly, aiming my weapon in front of me. I glance around the room, blood is everywhere, but so far there are no bodies.

"Mrs. Duncan, are you in here?" I ask, slowly creeping my way through the living room, avoiding stepping in the blood.

I peek into the hallway, pictures half hanging on the walls. Blood is smeared across the wall on the left, leading into the master bedroom. I sneak down the hall, peeking into the small bathroom as I pass. I quietly open the master bedroom door to see Mr. Duncan lying presumably dead on the floor.

Mrs. Duncan is sitting at the edge of the queen-sized bed, letting out shaky tears. She is still holding a small revolver in her hand, her hand quivering under its weight. I stay just outside the door, using the small crevice of wall for cover in case she turned the weapon on me.

"Mrs. Duncan." I say reassuringly. "I need you to put the weapon down, can you do that for me?"

She glances up at me, her eyes bright red as tears fall from them, pain and betrayal written all over her face.

"I'm sorry." She says, raising the gun to her temple.

"Wait!" I shout, but it's too late, she pulls the trigger and ends her misery. Blood is sent across the wall, soaking the family portrait on the bedside table. I stand there in silence as her body goes limp, then falls to join her husband on the floor.

I pull my phone from my pocket and dial 911, having them send the police and a coroner. I walk back outside and wait for them to arrive from my car. I look out at the horizon, watching as the sun sets. This would have been a wonderful day under different circumstances. The summer heat beats through the windshield. The silence breaking from approaching sirens in the air.

Another day in paradise.

2

stare at the ceiling as I lie in the cheap motel bed, water stains from years of neglect cover the white plaster. The old wallpaper is flaked away and tearing itself from the wall behind. The carpet has stains all over them from what I don't know, nor do I want to, ignorance is bliss.

I used to have dreams, used to want to be more than this. I work as a private investigator not because I want to, simply because I don't really have any other skills. I spent two years in the military, but that quickly ended after they suspected me of being a little crazy, not that they were wrong, but they weren't necessarily right either. Don't get me wrong, I am fucked up in the head, but I can still get a job done.

Shortly after my military career crashed and burned I turned next to the police force, I worked in a few small-town departments for around four years before I was terminated due to unnecessary aggressive methods. What a load, I was just doing my job. But I digress, here I am now, working the garbage cases no one wants or has the time to do. The pay is not worth the time, but basic self-employment is one of the few things I can manage to do.

I sit up on the bed, a few cases I'm considering working set sprawled out on the crappy wooden table in the corner next to a broken air condition unit. I walk over and plop onto the small chair by the table. I glance into the cracked mirror on the wall in front of me. Fuck, I look like shit. Dark circles enclose my eyes from sleepless nights. My long black overcoat drapes to the floor, I look more like a cultist than an investigator. My hair is slicked back at an attempt to seem a bit more professional.

Most of the cases are your basic crap, cheating spouse, missing pet, bullshit about drugs you name it. Even got a few on paranormal incidents, don't know why they would send that to someone like me, I'm no demonologist, but hey those cases can be interesting.

A few years back I took a paranormal case where an elderly woman believed her late husband was haunting her house, stating that he was angered by her selling the chair that he spent all his days lounging in. She went on to say that he was moving the curtains, knocking pictures off the wall, and made the television stop working.

As I investigated the house I quickly noticed she had a large box fan set up in her window, if you turn it on the wind it blows knocks her pictures down, and as the air circulates it moves the curtains on the other side of the room. Her television issue on the other hand was kind of funny, she simply had knocked the plug out of the socket, don't know why she never bothered to look. But one way or another she believed I had some kind of gift and thanked me for "banishing the spirit," I accepted her thanks but I did nothing more than point out the obvious.

I flipped through a few of the cases only one really caught my eye, it was one of the paranormal type of cases, but it had involved a more real basis, not that I don't believe in ghosts and all that, I have just never encountered any. But as I was saying, this case involved a string of murders and suicides all under unnatural or unexplainable instances. A lot of the suicides appear to be jumpers, no surprise. The strange thing beyond the deaths were that they all appear to be from the eighth floor. The string of deaths date back to the early 1900's, right around when the hotel building was built.

Eh, screw it I'll give them a call, might as well check it out. I pull my phone out and dial the hotel manager that sent me the case, a Mr. Clay. Guess he doesn't want to be on a first name basis.

"Thank you for calling Bloomingdale, how may I direct your call?" The voice on the other side said.

"Yes, I need to speak with a Mr. Clay." I say.

"One moment sir." They replied.

They woman put me on hold forcing me to listen to that irritating elevator music jingling in my ear.

"Mr. Clay speaking, what can I do for you?" He said.

"Yes, this is Jeff Barnes, I am a private investigator. You had contacted me regarding a paranormal string of incidents." I say.

"Oh, Mr. Barnes. Yes, thank you for responding so quickly." He goes on. "I would love to speak more on the matter but will not do so over the phone. Please meet with me at the hotel and we can discuss the matter further."

"Uh, alright. Give me an hour or so and I'll be there." I say.

"Good day sir." He said, hanging up on me.

That was something, I grab the case files and put them in a small briefcase to bring along with me. I walk over to the small mini fridge and pull out a small bottle of whiskey and down a few shots, the burn in my throat makes me wince.

I grab my car keys off the small table and head out the door. The Bloomingdale Hotel is around an hour from here, over in Taylor City. Hopefully this case is worth my time, not more smoke in mirrors.

3

I arrive at the Bloomingdale Hotel, it's around five pm, the warm glow of the sun cooks me as I pull into the parking lot. The place is enormous, tallest building in the city, at least seven hundred rooms. Giant windows cover most of the building, one for every room. On the top of the hotel you can just make out small gargoyle statues. The building seems to be trimmed in a shade of gold.

I make my way across the parking lot towards the front entrance. Cars flying this way and that, crowding up the city streets. Horns are honking in the distance, these small annoyances are one of the reasons I tend to stay away from cities, can't stand people.

A man is standing at the front door, using his hand to guide you in. He is some sort of butler I assume based on his attire. He is wearing a black tuxedo style suit topped off with a pair of white gloves, a red pin stripe shoots down his pant leg.

I enter the hotel; the lobby seems far too elegant to have such so called paranormal instances. It's almost sickeningly bright, everything a shade of gold or silver. Tall staircases on both sides of the lobby leading to a second floor. A set of at least ten different elevators line the hallway just behind the front desk attendant. Small golden statues are strung throughout, set on short pedestals. A giant fountain of gold and silver is centered in the room. Looks like a place a king or emperor would live, like a palace.

I approach the front attendant, as I glance around trying to make something of this place.

"Hello, I'm here to meet with Mr. Clay." I say.

The attendant looks me up and down, as if to say that I don't belong here. Which I probably don't, I'm not a classy man by any means.

"One moment sir, let me see if he's in." The attendant replied, as he picks up a phone nearby.

The attendant speaks quietly afraid I may hear what he's saying, he keeps looking me over as he mutters into the phone. He wraps up with, "yes sir, at once." Then he hangs up and looks back at me again. He clears his throat before speaking.

"Mr. Clay will be with you momentarily, please…" He points to a set of couches and chairs behind me. "Wait over there for him, and sir…" He waits for me to look back at him. "Don't speak to our clients please, this is a thriving business we are running here. We don't need you spooking them." He said.

I let out a small chuckle at the insult and walk over to the couch, I plop down, the couch is ridiculously soft, almost swallowing me whole. I don't understand how people could sit on these comfortably, no support what so ever.

I check my bag and my pockets to make sure I have all my equipment I may need.

"How are you enjoying your stay so far, Mr. Barnes?" A man says from behind me.

The sudden noise makes me jump a bit. I turn around to see a tall man in a three-piece suit, all black with a bright red tie tucked into the top piece. He has large framed glasses which cover his bright piercing brown eyes. He has his hair slicked over to the side, he walks with his hands clasped behind his back. This must be the man of the hour, Mr. Clay.

"Well so far, so good. So, what is it we need to discuss?" I say, hoping up from the couch.

"Come. We will speak in my office." He said, turning to lead the way.

I don't get what is so secretive about the subject, it's not like people don't know what has happened here, it was printed in several newspapers. I suppose I'll indulge him, let him try and cover up his buildings past, for now at least.

He leads me down a set of long corridors, all filled with fancy art works along the walls. Small statues of Gods and Goddesses of various descent on pillars throughout the walkway. The walls are white with a golden trim, the corridors smell musty as we go, like an old basement. The place feels even bigger on the inside, if you don't already know where you are you could easily become lost in the maze of hallways.

We arrive in front of a tall wooden door, a large five-point star is embroiled upon it. Small golden button like dots are spread around the star, it gives off the vibe of a cultist symbol, but hey, to each his own. Mr. Clay pulls a large skeleton key from his pocket and unlocks the door. This place must be ancient, still using that fashion of key.

The door swings open revealing the large office of Mr. Clays'. Tall bookcases fill every wall, mainly full of books, though a few shelves have jars placed upon them filled with various liquids and plants. Kind of looks like a science experiment of some sort.

A large gothic looking desk sets centered in the room, a tall work lamp is placed on the right side. A laptop rests on the desk beside a stack of papers. The lights are dim, giving the room an eerie glow.

"Okay Mr. Barnes." Mr. Clay said, letting out his breath. "We need you to investigate strange incidents we have had, all taking place upon the 8th floor. We don't know if it is simply a coincidental thing or something more. We have heard speculations of it being cursed as well as reports of entities tormenting our guests. We have had the floor closed off in recent years, but the questions remain to be answered."

"What kind of incidents are we talking about? I know of several suicides and murders, but what are the so called paranormal events?" I ask, doubting the validity of his stories.

He grabs a file off his desk and flips through several pages and pictures. He hands a stack of photos and documents to me. They detail several strange occurrences, guests have reported seeing a man in a suit floating through the halls screaming, as well as a woman in an evening gown that follows them into their rooms. Several pictures of ritualistic scenes are taken that give the impression of some form of satanic cult activity.

The list of specified incidents detailed as follows:

1930 – Satanic ritual items found near two men and three women who were poisoned in room 808

1937 – Man found overdosed on pills in chair of room 804

1938 – Woman found outside hotel, apparent to have jumped from the window of room 810

1943 – A man was found to have shot himself in the head, no suicide note was present in room 802

1944 – Man was found with his throat cut by a small razor in room 809

1963 – A married couple were both found poisoned in room 811

1971 – Family of four found all with a single stab wound to the abdomen in room 805

1980 – Reports of ghostly figure moaning in hallways.

1982 – Man reported to have been chased by a ghostly man in a suit from his room.

1982 – Man found drowned in bathtub in room 801

1985 – Ghostly woman was seen following guests in the hallway.

1986 – Anonymous report of satanic ritual assumptions in adjoining room.

"This is just a small list of the key incidents, some were not reported on to protect our image from the public." Mr. Clay said, raising his eyebrows.

"Okay, well, to fully investigate such accusations I will need a room on the eighth floor." I stated, glancing up from the document.

"Of course, Mr. Barnes do be careful. I myself have never encountered any of these entities or otherwise in my time here, but the idea scared me enough to stay away from that floor. So, just make sure to not be complacent." He said, in a dark faint voice.

His eyes were saying much more than his words, as if he intentionally left out some information. Maybe he doesn't want to spook me, I'm not sure at this point. I'm sure whatever these people think they seen has some reasonable answer.

Mr. Clay digs in the small drawer in his desk, he then pulls out an old rusty key, holding it up to the dim lights.

"Here." He said, handing me the small key. "This is the key to room 806, one of the few rooms on that floor without incident, so far that is."

I grab the small key from him, the key is covered in rust with its room number etched into the metal. I put the key in my pocket and begin towards the door.

"Hold on Mr. Barnes, you will need me to take you to that floor, the elevators won't stop there." He said.

I give him a crooked look. Jeez these people must really believe that floor is cursed. I laugh a bit to myself as I wait for Mr. Clay. He heads out the door, I trail behind him. He takes me down another set of corridors, then we head into a narrow stairwell leading up.

The stairwell is not designed in the same fancy style as the rest of the hotel, it is a basic cement stairway with black white paint covering the walls. We go up for what feels like an eternity. My legs getting weak around the fifth floor, my lungs are choking me. Man, I'm glad I quit smoking, I can only imagine this trek if I still did. I'm pulling myself up by the handrail at this point, trying to will my legs forward.

We finally make it to the door to the eighth floor, a giant steel padlock is chained around the door latch, another sliding lock is placed at the top of the door. They really didn't want anyone in here. Mr. Clay pulls a large key from his pocket and releases the chained lock. He then pulls the slide lock open. Another lock is in the door latch itself, he pulls a separate key from his pocket now. Jamming the key into the keyhole, he twists the lock free.

Mr. Clay waves me towards the door. "Have a pleasant stay Mr. Barnes, I hope to hear from you in the morning about your findings."

I nod as I push the door to the eighth floor open, I have to put a little heave into it for the door to give way. I walk into the hallway glancing around.

"Oh, I never caught your first name by the way." I say, turning to see that Mr. Clay had already disappeared.

The floor looks just as normal as any other place around here, the carpets are a bright red with a golden swirl design in them. The same small statues on pillars line the walkway. Prestigious art is hung ideally throughout the walls, the air has a strong musty scent from years of neglect. Spider webs have clung to the corners of the ceiling. I would like to say, I fucking hate spiders. I walk down the long hallway passing by the rooms remembering the incidents that have occurred in each of them.

So far, I have not seen anything of the so called paranormal nature. Just a basic rich guy hotel. I pass by room 804 and 805, then walk up to the door to 806. I pull the small rusted key from my pocket and slide it into the keyhole. I have to jiggle it a bit to wear off the rust before the lock gives way.

I swing the door open, half expecting something from the pictures, but no. It's just a normal room, not much different from the one I call home. That is, beyond the price to be here.

A painting of a dog herding horses hangs above the large queen size bed. A bright red and gold quilt is laid upon the bed, small chocolates have been placed on the pillows, no doubt rotten at this point. The carpet is the same red as the hallway. A giant screen television is attached to the wall across from the bed, definitely an upgrade from my hotel. A small table and chair set is placed in the corner near the air condition unit.

I walk about the room checking for anything unusual, the bathroom is almost the size of the main area. A huge shower with a dual shower head is on the far end, the toilet is so large it looks as if it could swallow me whole. A golden toilet paper stand is placed nearby, with the paper pointed at the end. Stacks of towels fill the shelves behind the toilet. Nothing out of the ordinary.

I walk back into the main area and fall onto the bed, I flip on the television for some background noise, place is too quiet. I grab my bag and pull out a few documents and photos, spreading them around the bed. Nothing to really do but wait.

After around twenty minutes of sifting through papers and reports I hop up. I walk over and inspect the small mini fridge by the television, small bottles of alcohol are lining the top of the fridge, a few sandwiches are on the shelves covered in mold and some kind of fungus, at least they are wrapped up. The sight makes my stomach queasy. I grab a few small bottles of several types of rum from the top shelf. I down the first two quickly, need to take the edge off a bit.

I plop back onto the bed, twirling an empty bottle in my hand. So far, I think this is just another case of smoke in mirrors, just with more hype behind it. People see what they wanna see, probably just imagined it. It could have even been a prank from some assholes.

It kind of feels like it is just one of those scenarios like you see on tv, you know like the people who go in and investigate the so called paranormal. They will be standing near an open window saying crap like, "did you feel that? It suddenly got cold here." Real lame ass shit like that. No shit it got suddenly cold there, you're by a window moron. Even better when they think the old creaking floorboards are some kind of ghost wandering around toying with them, um, no stupid it's you making that noise. Dumb shit like that, hard to think people believe them.

I look over at the tv on the wall, grabbing the remote I flip through a few channels, nothing much on. Several news stations pattering on about the same crap, old sitcom reruns, never anything on. I let out a sigh and walk over to the door. I look out into the halls to the left and right, half hoping to see something happening, the boredom is starting to give me cabin fever.

It's strange being the only person on this floor, the silence is so powerful it makes you uneasy. The lights of the hall are dimmed, a few flickering as if they are about to blow. I pull the door shut and turn back to the room. A loud thud shoots out of the bathroom, the sudden noise makes me jump. I slowly walk over to investigate the sound. I peek in seeing a small travel size shampoo bottle on the floor, must have fallen off the shelf. I bend over and pick it up, placing it back on its shelf.

I turn back, walking towards the main bed area. I plop onto the bed, regretting my decision to bother coming here. I look up and stare at the ceiling as I down another bottle of rum. A distinct creaking sound is heard from the hallway, I quickly hop up and sneak a peek into the halls again. Nothing.

As I turn to shut the door the tv on the wall begins to cut out, sending shockwaves of static across the screen before shutting off entirely.

"What a piece of junk." I groan.

I walk up to it and hit the power button but the tv doesn't respond. I give it a quick smack in frustration. Great now there is even less to do here. I turn towards the bed as the tv shoots on, the volume so loud I feel I will go deaf. I nearly jump straight out of my skin as I slam my hands over my ears. I turn and yank the power cord from the wall, tossing it onto the ground in frustration.

The room goes silent again as the tv shuts off. My nerves are a bit frantic at this point, the sharp sound of the tv had sent my adrenaline into overdrive. I run over to the door and look out into the hallway once more, needing some reassurance that nothing was still happening. The hallway has gone dark, not even the slightest glimmer of light. The sight of the complete darkness makes my heart begin to pound. I quickly shut the door trying to hold onto my disbelief, telling myself this isn't real, just my imagination flaring up.

I twist the lock on the door, trying to keep whatever may be in the darkness outside. My breath has become shaky, I quickly walk over to the window, looking down at the street below. Trying to grasp onto any normalcy going on in the world. The cars are flying by without a care, stoplights blinking, stopping the vehicles ascent. I stare down for a few moments, taking in the fresh air. Gotta get my head straight.

I close my eyes and take in a big deep breath. I freeze, I get a hair-raising feeling like something is in the room, watching me. That feeling creeps into my entire being, paralyzing me, afraid to turn, afraid what I may find. Panic rises in my throat making my breath shudder. A small click is heard behind me as the lights shut off in the room. I can't move, the urge to climb out onto the window ledge to escape is overwhelming.

I grit my teeth and slowly turn to meet my fate in the darkness. The room is pitch black, I can't see a foot in front of me. A sound like footsteps moves across the room, but I can't see what is making them. Then a deep growl of a laugh crosses the room, bouncing from wall to wall, engulfing the room. My heart is pounding so hard I feel it may rip straight out of my chest. The laughter is getting closer, closing in on me. I give in to the urge and jump over the window pane, clinging to the side of the building onto the window ledge.

Fear has completely taken me over, my body shaking as I shimmy away from the open window. I am moving too quickly my foot missteps nearly plunging me to the depths below, but I manage to cling on for dear life. The window of the room slams shut, so hard the glass shatters out, shards spray out into the night air.

I move farther away, trying to make it across to the next room over. Sweat is dripping down my face, the salty drops stinging my eyes. I make it to the next rooms window. I grip the building tightly as I bend down trying to open the window with my spare hand. It's held shut tight, I yank as hard as I can, it finally gives way, flying open so fast I lose my grip. I swing backwards, hanging on by one hand, the fall waiting for me. I swing myself back to the safety of the ledge and jump into the window.

I let out a sigh of relief as my feet are back on safe ground. I run over to the light switch and flip them on. This room is a mess, completely destroyed. The bed had been sliced apart by some kind of knife, the feathers of the pillow top strung across the floor. The table has been dismantled with one of its legs jammed through the tv screen. A large red stain is in the middle of the floor, almost as if this were a preserved murder scene. A large pentagram has been drawn on the wall in what looks like blood.

The room sends chills up my spine, the reality of the whole situation begins to set in on me. I have to get out of here. I begin heading towards the door, as a knock hits it from the outside. I freeze, slowly I step closer to the door. I glance out of the peep hole into the hallway. It's black, the lights of the hallway have not returned, whoever or whatever is out there is engulfed in the darkness.

I keep looking out the hole, waiting for any movement I may catch sight of. Nothing. I back away for a moment before taking one last look out, when I put my eye up to the hole, I see something move. Slight shifts in the darkness going this way and that. Then I'm hit with a shockwave of panic as whatever is out there looks in at me from the outside of the peep hole. A large black eye is staring through the hole at me. Peering into my very soul, a loud growling moan rumbles in through the door, taunting me.

I back away, as the doorknob begins to twist. I slam my body into the door holding it shut. The force on the outside pushing back, making the door pop open slightly before shutting again. It's toying with me, as if I'm its new plaything. I reach for the door lock as I try to brace the door shut. I bounce back and forth, fighting with the door. I push with all my might and quickly lock the door.

I take a few steps back, watching the door, not trusting it to stay shut. Whatever is out there pounds on the door violently, before letting out a growl of a laugh and vanishes. I peek out the peep hole one last time, the lights have finally come back on in the hallway. They are dim and flickering, but they are on.

I take a step back gathering my nerves, I have to make a run for it. Without further thought, I unlock the door and bust out into the hallway, sprinting for the stairwell. Then a loud chuckle followed by a voice makes my blood run cold.

"Come out to play, have we?" A ghostly growl comes from behind me. The lights flickering as if they are afraid to shine. I run as fast as I can. Doors to the rooms ahead begin opening and slamming shut on their own as I pass by. Then it's all over, the lights give out turning the whole corridor into a dark abyss. I can't see where I am going, I must slow down so I don't run into anything.

I place my hand on the wall, feeling my way down the long hallway. The doors are still flapping open and closed, misleading my brain to the location of whatever is in here with me. I don't know what or who it is, but I can feel it closing in.

The deep growls and giggles bouncing off the wall. Traveling around the hallway, even feels like it could be in front of me. I am in full panic mode at this point. I feel helpless in the pure darkness, the panic is so powerful, my body is shaking. I can barely move in fear of what may come, I can't see how much further it is to the stairs.

Footsteps join the symphony of door slams, creeping down the hallway towards me.

"Here kitty, kitty." The voice growls.

My legs are weak, I practically am crawling, praying for a glimmer of light to shine, even for just a moment. Something begins scraping along the walls, like a knife grinding on metal. It's right behind me, maybe just ten feet away. I force my legs to run, stumbling in the dark, one hand on the wall guiding my way.

"You can't hide from us." The voice giggled.

Us? There's more of them in here? I have to get to the stairs, have to get out. Then I see it, a small sliver of light shining under a door ahead, that must be the stairs.

I take every ounce of energy I have left and sprint through the blackness. I grab the door handle and bust out into the stairwell, the light hits me as if God himself has shined down into this hell.

I don't stop for even a second, sprinting down the stairs two at a time. I stumble nearly tripping down the flights of stairs, but I retain my balance. I make it to the bottom and burst through the door to the corridors of the main floor. The gold and silver of the main halls blinding me as I run down them.

I run out into the lobby, the customers all stop and stare as I sprint past them. The attendant at the front yells something to me, but all sound is muffled in my ears from the terror inside me. I don't stop, pushing the front entrance doors open, I run out into the parking lot and jump into my car. I fumble my keys around trying to put them in the ignition.

I twist the key and the engine roars to life, I stomp the gas making my tires squeal as I speed out of the parking lot as fast as I possibly can. I speed down the road and I don't look back.

5

I pull open the door to the hotel room I call home. I drop onto the bed and close my eyes. Sleep evades me, the stress of what I just lived through too fresh in my mind. I still don't know what was in there, maybe the stories were true, maybe it is haunted or cursed. Either way I will never go back there. I have half a mind to get in the car and drive as far away as I can.

I sit up in the bed looking around the dull, cheap hotel room. I've stayed here for about six months now, I know every inch of the place. But, something seems different. I can't quite put my finger on what it may be, but it feels wrong, surreal. I walk around the small room inspecting it, everything seems to be right where it should be, but something is amiss.

I glance in the small dirty bathroom, nothing to see in there. The small phone on the bedside table begins to ring. Probably management checking to see if I'm finally going to leave yet. I don't think they're my biggest fans. I walk over to the phone and take it off the receiver.

"Hello." I say.

"How have you been enjoying your stay Mr. Barnes?" The voice asks, but the voice is not coming from the young woman who manages this hotel. It sounds familiar, wait, it couldn't be… Mr. Clay? No, that's impossible, how would he get this number.

"Who is this?" I ask, my hand begins to shake.

"I told you, you can't hide from me." The voice growls.

I pull the phone away from my ear, panic reclaiming my body. The phone begins to melt to ash in my hand. The room is changing, taking form of the one at Bloomingdale. That's not possible, I made it out. The lights go black, my heart is pounding a cold sweat down my face.

A look around in the darkness, a small beam of light appears, illuminating the small table in the corner. A small handgun is placed upon the table, my handgun. I walk over to it and pick up the gun. It's loaded, a bullet already in the chamber. I point it around the room, aiming at shadows.

My mind is frantic, waiting for something to come out. My body trembles under the weight of the weapon. A low guttural voice comes from the darkness, laughing.

"That is meant for you." It growled.

This thing wants me to shoot myself, this is what caused all the suicides. Those people were pushed to it, that's why there were never any suicide notes, they didn't want this. I try to drop the weapon, but I can't. My hand feels like something is squeezing it shut, holding tightly to the stock of the gun.

My arm is forced up high, turning the barrel towards my temple. I fight to push my arm away, it's no use, it won't budge. My finger is ripped away from its resting place along the slide, forced onto the trigger.

The deep growling voice laughs as my finger begins to tighten on the trigger. I feel a small click under my finger, followed by a deafening explosive sound. My eyes wide open as I fall to my knees, I can't feel anything, can't breathe. Blood gushes out, spaying a mist across the ground.

A shadowed figure approaches, dressed in a black cloak. A shiny metal necklace hangs around their neck. I am fading fast; the last breath of air escapes my lungs. I hit the floor hard as blood pools around me. My eyes close as the world shuts down around me. I hear the last words as I fade into nothing.

"How was your stay Mr. Barnes?"

Then I was gone.

Haddix

2:04 A.M.

Ring…Ring…Ring… I opened my eyes to the terrible sound of the phone ringing. It felt as if the sound of the phone shook my entire body into consciousness. I glanced at the clock buried under a pile of clothes on my nightstand.

"2:04, who the fuck calls someone at this time", I said.

Ring…Ring…Ring… Slowly I make my way across the room, stumbling, trying to get my balance in the darkness.

"Hello", I said as I picked up the phone. Silence.

"Hello", I say again. Still silence. Annoyed from the unanswered call I slam the phone back onto the receiver.

I make my way back across the dark room to my bed, I fall into the bed and close my eyes.

Ring…Ring…Ring…

"Ah", I yell. I quickly run back to the phone, yank it up to my ear.

"Hey asshole, I don't know wha…"

A loud screeching static cuts me off, it screams into my ear like nails on a chalkboard.

"H…He…I need…" The voice is breaking up, I can't make out the words.

"What do you need?" I ask. My question is met with silence. I wait on the line for a few minutes. I hang the phone up. "Probably a prank or something", I said.

I go back to my bed and lie down and slowly everything fades to black.

6:00 A.M.

"**G**od, I feel like crap". I said as I opened my eyes to the sound of the alarm clock.

Shit, I don't know why I always set my alarm for six, I guess it's just for those last few minutes of sleep before I must go into the hell that is my job. I work at the local grocery store downtown. It's an old worn down building, when it rains the ceiling leaks, a real piece of junk. But, it always manages to be busy considering it's the only store in town.

I'm that guy sitting behind the cash register you see every day complaining to that we don't honor your stupid coupons there like I really give a shit you didn't get to save ten cents off your potato chips, I mean seriously get over it it's ten cents for God's sake. Yeah, I'm that guy.

We don't even have a twenty-four-hour gas station here. Practically live in the middle of nowhere.

I always planned to run away from this place, but I never quite manage to get out. It's as though this place is a giant traffic jam and the cars aren't moving anywhere. So, here I am, stuck in Bedford, working at the local shithole.

"Hey, Derek"

I look out the window and my buddy Marcus is outside yelling up at me. He's got his standard ripped blue jeans on, and an old hoodie he stole from our friend Cory. He also has his trusty camera he takes everywhere with him, always looking for a good picture or story to report on, he is a photo journalist for the Bedford Times.

"Get your ass down here, I got this awesome story I'm lookin into. You've gotta hear it" he said.

"Yeah, yeah, I'll be down in a minute".

He always has some story he just has to tell me, typically some crap like how old Mrs. Perkins broke her hip again, or how local law enforcement had to deal with loose cows, real dumb stuff that no one really cares to read about.

I dig through the mountain of clothes on my table and find a pair of black jeans and a black shirt that seem clean enough, I spray some body spray on them for safe measure.

I head down the hallway and grab a coke from the kitchen, gotta get that sweet caffeine in me before life happens today. I open the front door to see Marcus with this big goofy grin on his face, his thick dark blonde hair is all slicked back with greasy looking gunk on it.

"What's up Mark" I ask.

"Dude, I got this intense story the paper wants me to investigate on".

"Oh, yeah? What, did the school decide to go with the blue football jerseys this year instead of the white" I say.

"Ha, ha, real funny, this is a serious art you know people like to read my stories I give them".

"Sure, sure, well let's hear it then".

"Alright, you know that old sanatorium out by the old abandoned hospital?"

"Yeah, so" I say. "They want you do go interrogate the crack heads who live there?"

He holds up an old missing persons' newspaper clipping.

"See this, these people have been missing for years, I was hanging out by the police station and I overheard them saying they think there might be a lead on the missing people there. So, I told the Times and they want me to go in there and see if I can beat the police to the punch."

"So, let me get this straight you want to go into an old abandoned mental asylum and find leads on missing people? That's ridiculous, all you will find there are the crack heads and maybe a need for a tetanus shot". I say.

"Always nay saying, have a little faith man, this could be my big break to get noticed by big shots and get the hell out of this place".

"Ha, well good luck with that man". I laugh.

"Well either way I am heading over there in a few hours, you can join me if you want". He said.

"Nah, I think I will pass, I gotta get to work, plus I told Cory I would swing by his place after work".

He shrugs and turns to walk away. "Suit yourself, when I make it big remember you could have been a witness in my story". He said.

He walks off down the road snapping a few pictures of the houses next door. I walk over to my car parked out front by the curb. I hop in and start the engine. I let out a sigh of disgust, "Here we go".

3:30 P.M.

I hate this place. Nothing but assholes all day. If it's not the customers, it's my boss Dan. The prick sits on his fat ass all day in the office doing nothing, then preaches to me about all the crap I should be doing, as if I'm not already doing fifty things at once now. But whatever I doubt I'll stick around here for another week, I can't see how people can just settle for work like this when there is so much more out there.

Finally, four o'clock, time to get the fuck out of here. I walk across the store to the time card machine and clock out.

"Hey". I hear Dan yell from his office.

"Derek, come in here".

Shit, I knew I should have sprinted out of here. I walk over to his office and open the door, the door knob is slick with what is most likely pizza grease, the pig never stops eating. I walk in and see Dan sitting in his broken-down computer chair, worn down from years of his massive body crushing it to pieces. I can almost hear it screaming for air.

He is not my idea of a store manager, he looks more like someone you would see living in some trailer park, he's wearing an old ripped up white tank top, and some greasy stained blue jeans.

"What do you need". I say.

"Take out the trash in the bathrooms before you go, it smells like shit in there".

Smells like shit in here, I thought. He's sweating out some kind of nasty odors it's hard to breathe in here, kind of like when you pass by a power plant, that rotten eggs smell, ugh.

"yeah, sure, why not". I said.

I turn around and head out the door and walk past the cluttered aisles to the bathrooms. You can smell the urine odor before you even open the doors, probably because the lazy bastard hasn't had them cleaned in over a month.

The room is a mess, there is old pieces of toilet paper caked to the floor, and the toilets are as if someone decided to take a dump standing up, no attempt to make it in the bowl, it's sickening. I grab the trash cans and drag them out the back door to the dumpster.

I dump the trash cans into the dumpster quickly to avoid anything that may fall out on me. There is an old newspaper on the ground by the dumpster with more of those missing people pictures and articles on them, like Mark was showing me.

I wonder if he ever found anything over at the old sanitarium, unlikely. I thought.

I don't bother going back in the store in fear that there would be some other chore the fat man would want me to do, so I circled around the store back to my car to make a speedy exit.

I hop in the car and head out to Cory's place. He lives in one of those fancy big houses uptown, his parents are loaded so he's never really had to do any real work. Lucky fucker. It works out for him though, he has really bad social anxiety and the thought of going out in public is a panic attack waiting to happen. If it weren't for me and Mark, he would probably never leave his house.

Cory didn't always have an issue going out, it all kind of started when we were in high school. Cory got picked on by the Baker boys, they hated Cory, don't know if it was out of jealousy or just because he was an easy target. But, one day when Cory was walking home from school the Baker boys attacked him on the street. They got him pretty good, put him in the hospital for a few weeks. He had a few broken ribs, and a concussion from it, he's never been the same since.

I pulled up into Cory's driveway and cut the engine off. His place has an old gothic style to it, makes me think of a castle towering over me. I walk up and knock on the door, he has this cool door knocker on it resembling a dragon, real medieval looking.

"Who is it?" I hear Cory ask in a scared whisper.

"It's me". I yell.

Cory cracks the door open and peaks out at me. His house is dark on the inside, as if all their lights blew out.

"Oh, what's up man, forgot you were coming over".

"Nothing much, you gonna let me in?" I ask.

He opens the door reluctantly and lets me in. This place is ridiculous, filled with a bunch of random junk his parents collected over the years, kinda like a museum in here. Old paintings fill the walls, big stone stands with big vases on them. There is a big winding staircase going up in the middle of the room, like something you would see in a ballroom as someone important shows up. Too much space I would get lost in here.

"Hey, you hear from Mark today?" I ask.

He shook his head with a shrug. "Nah, not today."

Cory's wearing some old bath robe that looks like motel drapes and some house slippers, still in his pajamas. I guess Mark is still at the old asylum.

"So, anything fun happening over here?"

"Not really, I have been trying to trace this strange phone call I got today." He said. "Mostly static on the line, but it tripped me out, so I had to figure out who it was or if it was a prank or something."

"Did you figure it out then?" I ask.

I wonder if I should mention the strange call I got today, almost forgot it even happened. Then again, he would probably think it's some kind of conspiracy, he thinks the world is always trying to kill him.

"Well, I found a location on it to where it should be, but there are no buildings in the area, no phone booth, nothing. Doesn't make sense."

"Is it from Bedford, or...?" I ask.

"It showed it was somewhere just outside town, near the old hospital buildings." He mumbled.

"What time did they call you? It could have been Mark, he's up that way working on a story for the Times."

He shakes his head in disbelief.

"I have his number you know, plus that dude was definitely passed out when I got the call, it was like two in the morning."

I must have had a strange look on my face, Cory instantly looked panicked, as if he saw a ghost. He turned and ran up the stairs towards his room.

"What are you doing?" I yell up to him.

"One sec". He said.

This guy is always in such a panic it makes me feel nervous just being around him, like maybe he is right maybe the worlds out to get him and I'm gonna be taken out for being in the same area. The guys stressful.

I wonder if somehow the two calls are connected or just some coincidence, it couldn't have been Mark I seen him hours after I was called. I just want to blow it off as a wrong number.

Then again, maybe Mark was right and there are missing people up there, but how would they get my number. I guess they could just hit random numbers and see who answers but, that's a bit of a stretch since they called Cory too. See this guy's already in my head making me trip out and I've only been here like ten minutes.

Cory comes running out of his room, down the stairs holding a paper. He runs up to me breathing heavy, as if he just ran a marathon.

"Look". He says shoving the paper in my face. "missing people, there have been reports of them going missing near those buildings".

"I know, that's what Mark was going up there to investigate, he wanted to beat the cops to the punch on the story."

He shakes his head; his eyes are red like he hasn't slept in a month. He has his usual panicked expression on face, eyes darting around like someone might be listening in.

"What if that's who called, maybe they need help." He puts his hands on his head and starts breathing even heavier. "Or what about Mark, what if something happened to him. Oh, my God, Oh God."

"Calm down man, just call Mark, I bet he's fine, probably

interviewing all the crack heads up there. He could already be back home for all you know." I grab him by the shoulders. "Chill."

He reaches in his pocket and grabs his phone, almost drops it from his shaking.

"Okay, okay, I'm calling him." He whispers.

He paces the floor as he calls. The guy is a wreck, once the box of cereal he likes changed the picture on the box and he couldn't find it, he panicked and had a meltdown in the middle of the store, lucky for him it was my store and I calmed him down and helped him find the box.

"He's not answering!" He screams.

He is back in full blown panic now, shaking and pacing the floors, he starts crying.

"We have to go see if he's okay!" He demands.

"Dude, calm down, we can drive up and see if he's still there." I grab a hold of him. "You gotta chill out though."

He gives me a slight nod and whimpers a bit. He throws off his robe and runs up to his room to change his clothes.

God, this guy is going to be the death of me. I let out a sigh, and walk outside. Need some fresh air after Cory sucked it all out of the house. It's a dark cloudy day, smells like rain in the air. It's the beginning of spring so it's always raining, there is a bit of a chill in the air but I can't take another day wearing a coat, got to let my skin breath. I never cared much for wearing those big poufy winter coats, rather freeze.

A few minutes' pass and Cory comes running out, still in a bit of a panic, he runs up to my car and hops in the passenger side.

"Let's roll." He announces.

I walk over and hop in the car and start up the engine. Here we go, this is not how I planned to spend my day.

5:00 P.M.

Feels like we've been driving forever, I don't know how much more of Cory's heavy breathing I can take. The guy has been on everything from anti-depressants to antipsychotics but nothing works for him.

The roads have turned from pavement into this powdered dirt, the lines have all disappeared. There are tall trees enclosing the road from both sides making it seem darker outside than it should be. Real creepy stuff, feels like I'm driving in a horror movie. If that's the case I hope I'm the main character, Cory has no hope.

I can barely see ten feet in front of the car, even with my high beams on. The car bounces on every bump and hole. We are getting close enough you can almost see the gates to the asylum.

The trees are still bare from the winter towering over us with dead limbs pointing high in the sky. We pass by a sign stating we are approaching the Haddix Asylum. We pull up to the gates, they are chained shut to keep out intruders. The place has been shut down since the fire in 1900 that destroyed the place killing most of the patients.

"Look, there's Marks' car!" Cory yelled.

"See, he's still here, no worries." I say reassuring him.

"No, not no worries, we gotta go find him to make sure he's okay." He demanded.

I let out a sigh. Of course, that wasn't enough for him, now he wants us to go in there and be murdered by crackheads.

"Fine, but if we don't find him in ten minutes I am leaving with or without you." I say

"Fine."

We hop out of the car and squeeze between the bars on the gate, not very secure for trying to keep people in or out. We head up the little dirt path past the gate, it's littered with trash and broken bottles, no doubt left from some teenagers sneaking up here to have a party. There are old stone statues along the path depicting two babies with their arms drawn behind them as if they are being bound to the stone.

We go on a few hundred more feet and see an old broken down fountain with a stone dragon in the middle, it still leaked a green watery liquid from its mouth.

Finally, we reach the main building, there appear to be a few lights still on in the building, I wouldn't have though there would still be any electricity out here.

"There, that room with the light on. That has got to be Mark, right." Cory says pointing up at the lit room.

This place is creeping me out, it's so quiet out I can hear my heart beating in my chest.

"Fine, but let's make it quick, this place is trippy." I say.

We walk up to the entrance door, Cory turns the knob.

"It's locked, do you see another way in?" He asks.

I shrug. "I don't know, hold on."

I walk around the corner of the building, this place is a wreck, there are old broken water drain pipes hanging down everywhere. Most of the windows are busted out leaving glass shards everywhere waiting for someone to cut their feet on. Weeds are growing up the sides of the building into a few windows.

There are still bars on the windows that they used to keep the patients from jumping out to kill themselves. Scorch marks from the fire cover the old brick walls.

An old half busted fire escape hangs down from the roof. "There, we can go up that fire escape, that's probably how Mark got in." I say.

Cory runs around the corner to meet me by the broken fire escape. I cup my hands and help him up onto the stairs. I jump up and grab the bottom step and pull myself up cutting my leg on a broken piece of metal sticking out.

"Ah, shit!" I yell as a small trickle of blood runs down my leg.

"You good?" Cory asks

"Yeah, piece of crap old building is falling apart. Let's go, I'm already over this place."

We go up the escape stairs slowly, it's creaking and shaking with our every move. Feels like the whole thing is going to fall off at any second. I try to look in through the windows but they are too dark to see anything in. We go up four floors before we reach the roof. Cory is looks like he's about to drop dead from the climb, he never was much of an athlete but jeez it wasn't that many stairs.

"Finally, we made it to the top. I wasn't sure I was going to make it after the third floor." Cory said with all the breath he could manage.

"Yeah, now let's find Mark and go." I said.

My leg is still bleeding leaving a trail like breadcrumbs behind us. There is chunks of ground missing on the roof, giant holes waiting to swallow you into the darkness. The roof access door has been completely removed from its hinges, thrown across the ground in pieces.

There is more trash and bottles up here as well as scorch marks and some kind of orange looking stain splattered around the roof. Looks like a murder scene.

"Well, on the plus side, this door isn't locked eh." I said.

"True." Cory responded.

Cory reached into his pocket and pulled out his phone. He pressed a button and turned on a flashlight.

"There, now we won't be going in here blind." He said.

"Okay, lead the way then." I said waving my hand toward the doorway.

"No wait, here, you take it." Cory said handing me his phone.

I walked up to the doorway and shined the light into the darkness illuminating a small staircase.

"Come on." I say.

We walk down the stairs into the top floor of the building. There is a strange smell in the air, like the smell of dead animals, probably from whatever rodents made this place their home. A small glint from old dangling lightbulbs gave a dim light to the hallway in front of us.

We walk down the hall slowly, unsure yet how strong the floors still are here. The paint on the walls are burnt and chipped away. The same orange looking stains are splattered along the walls.

"What has been going on here?" Cory asks touching the walls.

"I don't know, but I'm not a fan of their decorating." I smirk.

There are old bathtubs ripped from their homes, thrown out around smalls rooms to our left. A stray wheelchair sits in the middle of the hallway. The smells are getting stronger the further we go.

"God, I think I'm gonna be sick, what is that smell?" Cory said.

We go on down the hall, more bathrooms and shower areas are in the small rooms to our left.

"What was that?" Cory asks.

"Shh." I say.

We listen quietly, a small muttered sound is coming from the room on the far right of the hallway. We slowly move to peek into the room. The smell is right on top of us now, choking you, it's so strong. The sound is getting closer as we approach the room.

"Don't look at him." The voice says. "Don't look."

"Don't look at who?" Cory asks me.

We peek around the corner of the doorway. There is a person standing in the corner of the room, facing the wall.

"Shine the light in there, I can't see anything." Cory said.

I lift the light up to see into the room.

"Holy shit, it's Mark, that's my hoodie he stole." Cory declared.

"Hold up, are you sure?" I ask.

"Dude, I would know that jacket anywhere, look at the hole in elbow. I did that last week messing around in my room." He said.

"I don't know man, why is he just standing there like that."

Cory shrugs his shoulders and walks into the room.

"Mark, what the hell are you doing?" Cory questioned.

The man turned slowly around to face him.

"Oh, what the fuck!" Cory yelled stepping backwards.

Cory slowly walked backwards away from the figure, the man started towards him. I took a step forward so my light would reach them.

The man then leaps forward at Cory tackling him to the ground screaming.

"Don't look at him, don't look!" The man screamed.

"Get the fuck off me psycho!" Cory yelled back.

I ran up and pushed the man off Cory, I pull him to his feet and back up a few feet. I shine the light at the man.

"Oh, my God." I said.

The light revealed the man, he stood there still, his clothes in shreds with blood covering them. I froze staring at him, my heart now pounding through my chest. I feel as if I'm paralyzed. The mans' face is covered in cuts, and his eyes have been removed, there is dried blood running down his face like tears. He keeps muttering the same phrase over and over.

"Don't look at him, don't look." The man repeats.

I grab Cory by the arm and pull him away.

"We have got to find Mark and fast, I don't know what the hell is going on around here and I don't want to find out." I declare.

"I second that." He responds.

We run down to the end of the hallway, there is a staircase down to the next level. We quickly make our way down the stairs, Cory nearly tripping over himself, he's in panic mode again, for good reason this time. I'm right there with him at this point, I can't even think straight. I know I don't want to run into whoever or whatever did that to that man.

"There." Cory says pointing.

We see the lit-up room we've been looking for. We run past a few empty rooms with the windows broken out of on our right, then a couple on our left that appear to be some kind of medical areas.

"I think we're in the infirmary." I say.

"Yeah, maybe."

We continue down the hall till we reach the bright lit room. There is an old operating table under a giant surgical light. The table is covered in blood, it's still dripping off the sides onto the floor, creating a pool.

There are strange homemade tools on the counters covered in blood and chunks of skin. A saw blade is laying on the floor with what looks like hair stuck in it.

"Jesus, you don't think…?" I start.

"No, no it can't be." He said.

Cory's face was pale with complete fear, shaking, he begins to pace the room.

"Hey, is this…?" Cory asks.

I walk over to see he's holding Marks' camera.

"That's Marks', he never goes anywhere without it. You don't think that blood is from him, do you?" I ask.

"I hope not, I mean there's no body here, he could have just seen this mess and rushed out of here."

"Yeah, maybe." I said quietly.

I don't know none of this makes sense, I thought this was just some missing persons tip, not a full-blown murder scene. How does no one know what goes on here?

"Hey, let me see that camera really quick." I say putting my hand out.

I wonder if he managed to take any pictures that could tell us where he is. I turn the camera on, his battery light is blinking. I shuffle through a few pictures he took this morning by my place. Just houses and random people around town. He took a few of the gates here, there are a few snap shots of the main building from the outside.

Wait, who is that, there is a picture of a man wearing a surgical mask pointing at something, another of some kind of nurse, I think. But, they look odd, as if they went through a time machine, their clothes are really outdated and covered in that orange stain. The nurse has that old red cross symbol like medics wore in like world war two or something on her hat, surreal.

The last picture he took was this room, he took a picture of the bloody table, and the saw blade. On the plus side, I guess that shouldn't be his blood, but who were those people, and where did he go. I have way too many questions and no answers.

"Hmm, these don't really tell us much, but there are some strange people Mark ran into at some point in here." I say.

"Let's keep looking for him." Cory said.

We turn to leave the room and head back out into the hall, this floor seems to have power, most of the lights that remain on this floor are all turned on. There are small drops of blood along the floor leading to several rooms. We glance in a few as we go down the halls, hoping to find some trace of Mark.

The same smell as the floor above is in the air as we go down the hall. It gets stronger as we go, it seems to be coming from the room just ahead of us. We move slowly, hoping we don't run into anything like the man upstairs. We peek into the room the smell is coming from.

Jesus, is this real? There is a small mountain of dismantled small animals, cats, dogs, some sort of rodents, all cut into pieces. Cory turns white at the sight of it. He begins choking on the fumes and dry heaving. My heart is pounding, speechless. The smell is so strong it's all I can do not to throw up. There are jars along the counter filled with different types of eyes suspended in liquids.

Then I see it, there is a small piece of paper beside the mountain of corpses. I hold my breath, trying not to take in any more of the smell as I approach the note. There are fly's and maggots everywhere, enjoying their new homes. I quickly grab the paper and back away.

The note looks like a page out of Mark's notepad, it reads.

2003March21

10:00 a.m.

I arrive at the gates to the Haddix Asylum, I am here researching a lead on the missing people of Bedford, Iowa. It is currently daytime, though the light doesn't seem to reach here. I have been sent to find clues regarding the missing people for the Bedford Times, the police have been receiving phone calls stating that those people have been sighted in the area. So far, I have not spotted any of them, I am going in for a closer look.

10:07 a.m.

I arrive at the main building, the windows are all barred, and the doors are all locked from the inside. I find a fire escape and make my way to the top floor. I come across a few old syringes on the roof, unlikely related to the missing persons. I have noted an orange stain on multiple surfaces as I go. The floors are dark, but quiet. No sign of the missing people.

10:25

I have continued my search, finding nothing but old bathrooms and medical waste. I have noted a pile of dead animals, most likely from some deranged drug addict previously in the area. I have not yet encountered anyone to question further on the matters at hand.

10:43

As I continue searching for any evidence, I came across some old clothing that appears to match a description of 10-year-old Anna Ducrane, a young girl that went missing last October. It looks like it was forced from her, but there is no sign of blood on it.

11:02

I have reached the second floor of the building; no sign of life is yet to be seen. This floor is set up in a different fashion, it has gates on all the doorways, I believe this is where the patients rooms were located. The rooms are empty beyond small tables in the corners and small beds. Most of the tables are broken and the beds are overturned or burned by the fire.

11:36

I encountered a strange man dressed up in surgical gear calling himself Dr. Vincent, he had a woman dressed as a nurse alongside him. They told me they were here to cleanse the filth from me, the man grabbed at me trying to hold me down, I kicked him and tried to run. They cornered me in the second-floor stairwell and the nurse injected me with something. I managed to fight them off and sprinted up to the next floor and hid under a small table in one of the rooms.

11:50

I can hear them looking for me. They are going through the rooms throwing things around. I don't know what to do, I'm fucking scared. I think they are going to kill me.

12:00

I can hear a new voice muttering words down the hall, the so-called doctor grabbed him as he screamed.

12:03

I can hear them sawing into the man they grabbed, the sounds are unbearable. The poor man is being tortured in there, but I can't help, I just can't, if I move I'm dead too.

12:39

I heard the doctor leave the area, so I muster up all the courage I can and go into the room the sounds were coming from. There is a table covered in so much blood, my stomach turns. There are chunks of skin and hair covering the tools they used on him. I know the man suffered. I snapped a picture of the scene. I gotta get out of here.

12:42

I think they are coming back, I have to....

"Oh, my God, we gotta leave man, like right now." I declared.

My whole body is trembling, I can't begin to believe what Mark had written. I don't know if he made it out or not, but something happened to him. I feel cold as ice with fear. The hairs on my neck are frozen in a panic.

I look up to meet Cory's eyes, but he stands there frozen, not blinking, staring behind me. He lifts his hand slowly to point at something. I turn my head slowly, feeling the presence of whatever is behind me. Then before I can even see it, it speaks.

"Little cows come out for slaughter, did they." The voice says in a deep growl.

The words cut straight through me like a knife. Then I feel it through all the panicked adrenaline, it wasn't the words. I look down and see it, a gush of blood shot from my side as a knife cuts straight through my hip. I try to scream in pain, but the words won't come out.

"No!" Cory screams.

I fall to my knees and try to crawl away, blood splashing below me. Cory picks up a brick off the ground, that had fallen off the broken walls. He throws it at the man with the knife, smacking him in the head. The man isn't fazed by the hit, but it gave me enough time to get back to my feet and run over by Cory.

We stand there in pure terror as the man approaches us. We go around the side of the mountain of carcasses, as he circled around towards us. We have but a small second to run to attempt escape. There is no way to fight him off. The man is a giant, he is at least six feet tall, and broad with muscles big enough to crush us with one hand. He raises his blade and slashes it at us as we sprint as fast as we can by him.

My breathing is pounding out of my chest as I run, I can't even feel the hole in my side, I'm so scared all I can think of is I have to get away.

"In there!" Cory yells directing me into a room to our left.

He drags me into the room and pushes me under a desk that is sitting overturned in the room, as he climbs into a small locker. My heart is pounding so hard I fear it's going to give away my location.

The man is going through the hallway kicking open doors, searching for us. I can hear him screaming.

"You little calves can't hide from me! I will find you!"

He goes up and down the hall yelling and breaking things. I hear him growling out small laughs as he hunts for us.

Then the sounds slowly get farther away, I can still hear him giggling as he walks away. Then he yells one last thing to us.

"Don't worry little piggy's, the doctor will be with you shortly."

The words sent a sharp chill into my veins as I remembered the notes from Mark we found. Then he is gone, for now. I try to calm my breathing so that he won't hear me and come back to finish the job.

"Fuck!" I whisper.

10:30 P.M.

We stayed there unmoving for twenty more minutes, we were too scared, too frozen in place. There is now a small pool underneath me soaking into my clothing from the knife wound. My adrenaline has subsided and the pain is searing through my entire body, but I dare not make a sound.

Cory slowly opens the locker and crawls out over to me.

"Are you okay, man?" Cory asks.

"Yeah, don't worry about it we gotta get out of here." I say cringing with pain.

He pulls me out to my feet, throwing my arm over his shoulders to help me walk. Every step shoots a jolt of pain into me. We make our way up the hallway to the staircase, we start up it back to the top floor. I stumble and fall on the stairs, letting out a groan of pain.

I get back up and lean into Cory, finally we make it to the top.

"Hold on, man." I say. "Give me a second."

He sits me up against the wall. It's getting harder to breath, he sits down next to me. It's pitch black in the hallway, can't even see his face sitting beside me. I reach into my pocket to grab the phone for light, but it's gone.

"Shit! I think I dropped the phone running from that guy." I say.

"Don't matter man, we're almost out of here." He responds.

We sit in silence for a few minutes as I try to catch my breath. Then I hear Cory start whimpering, I can understand he's scared. I'm scared. This whole thing is a nightmare.

"I'm so sorry man." He says.

"For what?"

"For dragging you here. I should have just calmed down, and let the police do their jobs. I'm so sorry, this is all my fault." He cries.

"It's okay man, I offered to bring you here, plus you were right, Mark was in trouble." I say reassuring him.

"Yeah, but now we still don't know what happened to him and we are in trouble. I mean look at you, you got stabbed because of me."

I sit there quietly, nothing I can tell him right now will make him feel better. We just have to focus on getting outside to my car, then we can leave this whole mess behind us, and send the police. Hopefully they find Mark and he's okay.

The hallway is completely silent, it's unsettling, but silence also means we're alone. I sit and wait for Cory to calm down before we move, I close my eyes and let myself drift away from this place. I think of the sunshine of the summer to come, remembering how my mother would always take me on long road trips to new places, she wanted me to really take in all the things the world had to offer.

The sunshine always got her going, she liked to take me on long hikes through the mountain trails she would find. It was a tough climb to the top, but once you reached it, you really felt good. As if the whole planet just stops for that one moment of peace just for you. We would stand there for a few minutes just letting the sun hit us as we took in the chilly breeze of the wind.

Standing on the top of those trails made you feel small looking out at the trees below, reminding you that there is so much more than yourself out there. Wish I was there now.

11:00 P.M.

snap back into reality, and grab Cory's shoulder.

"You good?" I ask.

"Yeah, let's go"

We stand back up and walk slowly, we avoid the room with the eyeless man. We make our way to the roof access stairs and start our climb up to the top. We get to the roof and pause taking in the feeling of freedom, somehow just being outside felt safer, like we were home free.

I limp my way to the fire escape right behind Cory, I grab onto the railing to balance myself out for the descent. We make our way down the winding stairs, they seem never to end.

Finally, we make it to the bottom, Cory hops down first, then helps me off the deathtrap. The ground feels soft, safe. Rain is pouring down from the sky, small glimmers of lightning light up the sky. You can hear the low rumble of thunder.

We start down the small dirt path to the gates, passing by the fountain, and stone statues. The gates are now within view, I start to feel a bit of excitement in the anticipation of being back in the car.

We make it to the gate and squeeze between the bars. I open the door to my car and hop in, Cory hops into the passenger seat. I turn the key and the engine roars into action.

"Alright, the roll." I say feeling relief.

"Hell yes!" Cory responds.

"Going somewhere?" A male voice says from the backseat as I feel a needle enter my neck.

There is a female laughing as she sticks one into Cory, then the world slowly fades to black.

I had a dream, you know one of those dreams where you know what you need to do in them, but it's as if some force is pushing against you, refusing to let you do what needs to be done.

That's how I felt, in the dream I see this woman, she is screaming in a room, screaming for help. I am outside the door looking in, the room is a blinding white. I stand in this hallway, like that of a school, there are lockers and water fountains to my left and right with no end in sight.

I see the woman screaming, I want to open the door and go help her but my hand can't grab the doorknob. I push my hand towards it but I can't get it, I try and try, never making it to the doorknob.

Suddenly the woman screams louder but at me like it's my fault I won't help her. I keep trying to open the door but the knob refuses my hand. Then the screaming stops. I look up to see her and she is directly in front of the door staring straight into my eyes, like she can she right into me.

It goes quiet for what feels like an eternity, then she turns away going back to the center of the room. The whole room bursts into flames making their way to her. I fight the door begging it to let me in, but I can't. The woman catches fire and just holds her gaze on me, silent. Then she's gone.

Only after it's too late does the door give way and let me in, but there is still nothing I can do.

12:45 A.M.

I awoke to the sounds of someone talking. I opened my eyes, it took a minute to focus. I looked around trying to make out the figures in the room. I could hear a man and a woman talking about some experiment.

I can see a metal table in the room, with a white sheet draped over it. There is an assortment of sharp instruments nearby on a cart. I can almost make out the people. I can hear Cory crying somewhere in the room.

Then I see them, it's that man and woman from the pictures Mark had taken. The man in surgical gear and the nurse. That must have been who injected us in the car.

"We were out! We were out!" I hear Cory scream.

"You were never out sweetheart." The woman says.

The man walks around the room picking up tools and mumbling. He shakes his head.

"This patient isn't responding to our group therapy." He says pointing at Cory

The nurse giggles and shrugs her shoulders with a grin.

"Guess we will have to try more drastic techniques." She suggests.

"Ah, you may be right Ms. Percival." He laughs.

The man grabs a straight jacket and tosses it to the woman.

"Here, prep the patient, we don't want him moving, that could be quite dangerous for him, ha." The man says with a crooked smile.

The woman walks over to Cory and straps him down in the straight jacket. Cory is screaming and crying.

"Let me go! Get off me!" He cried.

"Don't worry sweetie this will all be over soon." She said.

My heart is pounding, I can't move. I look down to see there are straps bounding me to a chair. I shake and move all I can trying to break free, but the straps don't budge.

"Now, now, we will be with you shortly, no need to get anxious." The man said.

They grab Cory and throw him onto the metal table. They put restraints across his body, Cory is shaking and screaming in panic. I can't do anything but watch.

The woman picks up a pair of rusty scissors and starts chopping off his hair. The man puts his hand in a jar full of orange liquid, then rubs his hands together. He picks up an old tool that looks like a type of drill. He cranks the drill with his hand and the bit on it begins to spin.

Cory is writhing on the table, screaming. The man stands over him then pauses.

"Oh my, we can't be having that now." He says squinting his eyes at Cory.

"You shouldn't have done that boy. You must never look at the doctor when he's working." The woman warned.

The man put down the drill and grabbed a circular tool with blades on it. He walked over to Cory and gave a quick smile.

"No, no, no, no, no!" Cory screamed

The doctor jams the bladed tool into Cory's eyes, yanking them out one by one. I slam my eyes shut so tight it hurts, I can't watch this. I hear the nurse drop his eyes into a liquid jar.

"Oh, these will make a nice addition, such a pretty brown color." The nurse laughed.

I hear Cory screaming in agony, hoping for death.

"That's better." The man says.

I hear the drill start spinning again, I peek open my eyes. Blood is spurting out of his eye sockets, running down to the floor. The doctor pushes the drill up against Cory's head and starts cranking it as Cory shrieks. The drill enters his skull sending blood across the room splashing into my face. The nurse is dancing around the room giggling.

Cory is no longer making any sounds; his body is shaking like he's having a seizure. I watch as he shakes and goes lifeless. I just stare as if it's all a dream I'm going to wake up from at any minute, like this nightmare is all in my head. I hope to wake up but, no peace ever comes.

I sit there in shock as they rip Cory apart, taking each limb from him, putting chunks in jars and throwing organs in a pile on the counter. I watch for an eternity.

The doctor then points at me, I quickly close my eyes, hoping he won't take them.

"Him, send him to the therapist!" He demanded.

The nurse giggled as she unstrapped me and threw me in a wheelchair. I peeked open my eyes, she was pushing me through a set of double doors, down a long lit up hallway. I passed by several rooms, each filled with other victims of their practice. I see a few I recognize from the missing persons list.

We continue down the long hallway through another set of doors, the lights are dim in this hallway. The rooms appear to be old offices, tables are flipped over in them, old debris is strung out across the floors. We must be on the bottom floor, I can see the entrance door as we pass by.

The woman begins to giggle again as we go into a small office room. There is an old ripped up couch against the wall, a small rotting desk table across from it. She puts the wheelchair up against the couch and smiles at me, her teeth are yellowed, what's left of them that is. Her breath is hot against my face with an unsettling odor coming from it.

She gives one last grin as she dances out of the room.

1:00
A.M.

I set there in silence for a while, waiting for whatever nightmare is to come next. If they did that to Cory I can only imagine what happened to Mark, or what will happen to me. No, I can't think that way. I shake my head trying to erase the thought, like my brain is an etch-a-sketch I can just reset.

There is a small clock ticking away on the desk. I stare as the minutes' turn. I look down and realize she never strapped me into the wheelchair, now is my chance, I gotta run for it. I'm about to stand as the door opens.

A tall thin man dressed in a ragged suit walks in, he has large framed glasses on, the lenses are so large his eyes are magnified inside them. His jet-black hair is greased back, he seems too clean to be in this place. Maybe he is one of the good guys, I don't know, I can't trust it to be true.

He gives me a quick smirk as he sits at the desk, he clasps his hands together, staring at me. He looked at me as if I was the crazy one here, like he was waiting for me to jump up and attack him.

He glances down at something on his desk and grabs a pen. He begins scribbling something on a piece of paper in front of him. I'm struck with complete confusion.

"What's going on?" I ask.

He holds up a finger to silence me. He makes a clicking sound with his mouth.

"Derek, is it?" He asks.

I nod in confusion. How does he know my name?

"Tell me Derek, how are you feeling this evening?" He questions.

I stare at him, my mouth open unable to find words.

"Derek?"

"I'm fine?" I say unsure how to respond.

"Fine you say, are you sure?" He says.

I nod again. His eyes are staring at me now, they're dark, cold as ice, piercing through me.

"Derek, you can be honest, this is a safe place." He claims.

Yeah, real safe, murdering psychos around every turn, I feel as safe as ever. I just watched my friend be ripped to pieces, but oh everything will be okay because this guy says it's safe.

"Who are you?" I ask.

"Me? I'm your psychiatrist Dr. Krane, you know that. We have been seeing each other for the last six months, remember?" He said.

Six months? This guy is insane, I have never seen him before in my life, let alone for six months. He smiles at me again, as if he sympathizes with how I am feeling.

"Listen Derek, you have been an inpatient here at Haddix for almost a year now. You came in and self-admitted yourself for treatment here. We have been working with you through a series of medications and talk therapy. Are you remembering? No? Well, as you know you were diagnosed with multiple personality disorder." He goes on.

There is no way, he is just trying to get in my head.

"You're lying, I have only been here for a few hours." I declare

"Now Derek, we have been through this, you only believe that because your personalities are shifting, yesterday when we met you had named yourself Mark, last week your name was Cory, how much of what you know can you really say is real?" He insists.

"I am not Cory or Mark, I know who I am, you fucking psychopaths ripped Cory to shreds just an hour ago, God knows what you've done to Mark, but you will all pay for this!" I shout.

"Fine, if you are going to be this way, I feel we may have to take another path with you, after all this time you still fail to cooperate with the easy methods of treatment!" He attests.

He stands and starts towards me.

"Nurse! Nurse! Come take this patient away, the doctor can deal with his instabilities now!" He shouts furiously.

I only have one shot, I must move now. I leap from the wheelchair, adrenaline rushing through my veins. I shove Dr. Krane back into the desk and blow open the door, I don't know where I'm going I just know I have to run and not stop.

I hear Dr. Krane shouting behind me, the nurse is running down the halls after me. I dart through a set of doors busting into another hallway, patients in the rooms on both sides are screaming, I just keep running.

I hear the doctor yelling as he starts up an engine. I can hear the buzzing of a saw in the distance. My heart is beating through my chest, my lungs exploding, just keep running.

I go down the hallway, there, the entrance door. I sprint up to it throwing my entire body at it, praying it gives way to me. It lets out a splintering burst as I plow through it.

I sprint across the courtyard, there's a small building in the distance. I run quickly to the building, not wasting any time I push through the front door. It's pitch black. I feel the walls searching for anything, I trip over a chair on the floor, stumbling, I make my way through the room, I bump into what feels like a bed. I get down on my hands and knees and slide underneath it, waiting.

There are spider webs everywhere, now covering me. I lay on the floor, still, silent. My body is trembling, my heart is beating so fast I feel like it may give up on me.

I hear the faint sounds of the doctors' saw grinding away, waiting to taste my flesh. My eyes begin to adjust to the darkness, I think I'm in a radio control room or security office. Maybe I can manage to get a message out to the police.

I can see an old model radio on a table across the room, there is a monitoring system nearby with the cables all ripped out. I slowly slide out from under the bed, crawling my way over to the table. I reach up trying to grab the handset on the radio.

Got it, now I just need to switch it on. I reach up again to flip the switch on. I hit it and it lets out a loud static yell.

"Fuck!" I shout.

I quickly reach up and twist the volume to near inaudible. I crawl back across the floor and under the bed in case I was heard. I waited for someone to come barreling through the door, but no one came.

I slide back out from under the bed and crawl back to the radio. I reach up and twist a knob, trying to find any frequency to call out to. I twist it till the static stops.

"Hello? Is anyone there?" I whisper.

The radio is silent, I twist the knob again, more static. This is hopeless I thought. I try twisting the knob one more time.

"Hello? Is anyone there? I need help." I whisper again.

I am met with more silence. I can hear the doctor nearing the small building, his saw blade whirling. I peek up out a small window above the radio. There he is, heading my way, the nurse is right behind him.

Quickly, I crawl across the floor, under the bed. Shit, they are sure to find me here. There is nowhere to hide, nowhere to run. I'm trapped.

They kick open the door, it smashes into the wall. Smoke fills the room from his saw engine. His eyes are scanning the area, the nurse giggling with an evil smile.

"He has to be in here somewhere!" The man shouts.

Static shoots from the radio, then a voice breaks through the static.

"Hello? Are you there?" The voice over the radio says. "How can I help?"

The doctor smashes his saw blade into the radio, sending sparks flying everywhere. Damn it, that was my only hope. I lay there as still as possible, praying they leave. The doctor turns his attention back around the room.

His eyes are black as night as he studies the room for movements or sounds. The nurse is searching the room, looking under the table, opening a locker in the corner. It's only a matter of time.

"Over here!" I hear someone shout.

The doctor turns and heads out of the room. The nurse heads to the door and pauses. She turns back around for one last look. She is looking right at me, our eyes meeting. Shit, I'm screwed.

She gets a huge evil grin on her face, she starts towards me. She gets down on her knees and pokes her head in, inches from my face.

"Well, hello there sweetie, did someone go for a stroll?" She says with a growl.

She reaches her hand in to grab me. I throw the bed up, slamming it on top of her, I leap over the bed and out the door. I am running with every ounce of energy I can muster. The doctor turns to see me running, his saw roars back to life.

I run back past the main building, around the corner and leap onto the old fire escape, clinging to the bottom stair for dear life. I quickly pull myself up as the doctor closes in on me. He swings his saw blade at me, cutting deep in the back of my leg.

"Ah!" I scream in agony.

Blood pours from my leg spraying out behind me, I crawl up the stairs trying to escape the doctor. He leaps up to grab onto the bottom stair, the nurse on his heels. I turn and kick him, trying to delay his ascent. He falls off the stairs and slams into the dirt his saw blade escaping his clutches and whirls down to meet him. It slams into his chest blades spinning, it tears into his chest sending a pool of blood flying into the air.

I sit there and watch as the saw rips through his chest, ending his existence. The saw blades whirl to a stop as the doctor lays lifeless. The nurse stares at him as he goes, then she smiles and turns back to me.

"My turn." She squeals.

She yanks the saw blade out of his chest and turns around heading around the corner. I quickly crawl up the stairs to the roof, hoping my way through the doorway back to the top floor. I have to find Cory's phone.

I sprint through the halls as fast as my leg allows, passing room after room, searching for the phone. I scale the stairs down another floor, it has to be here somewhere. I can hear the nurse approaching on the floor below me, laughing.

I search through the room Cory and I had hidden in earlier, nothing. The nurse is closing in on me, I hear her coming up the stairs.

There, there it is, laying on the ground near the doorway. I quickly run over to it, stumbling to get my footing. I grab it and head back up the halls, trying to put distance between the nurse and me.

My lungs are giving out as I sprint up the stairs to the top floor, I go down the never-ending hallway to the stairs up to the roof. I quickly hop onto the fire escape. I'm halfway down, almost there.

My leg locks up, knocking me off balance, I stumbling crashing into the metal stairs. I tumble down and fly off the bottom hurdling towards the ground. I smash into the dirt as the impact steals the breath from my lungs.

I lay their paralyzed from the impact. I try to move, but I can't breathe. I can see the nurse walking down the stairs above me, smiling that evil smile. She locks her sights on me.

I roll over to my stomach as I crawl away, my lungs only giving me shuttered breaths. I make it to my knees and then my feet. I limp as I go. I head down the path towards the gate, the nurse not far behind. I pull the phone out as I go, dialing 9-1-1.

I can almost see the gate, I hear the phone as it answers my call.

"9-1-1, what is your emergency?" The phone asks.

"Help me! I'm at the Haddix Asylum, they're trying to kill me!" I shout.

I stumble as my leg begins to give out, dropping the phone, no time to go back for it, I hope they heard me.

I am right up on the gates, I squeeze through the bars, throw open my car door, I don't hesitate, I quickly slam my door shut and fire up the engine. The nurse is coming between the gates' bars. I slam it in reverse and stomp on the gas.

She is sprinting at the car swinging the saw blades. The saw grinds the hood of the car, tearing through metal, but I dare not stop, I can't go back there. She starts sprinting again towards me, quickly closing the distance.

I am shaking so badly I can barely see straight, the blood loss is making me lightheaded. I try to focus on her as I keep backing up. She stops and throws the saw at the car, blades spinning as it flies.

I clench my eyes shut as it crashes through my windshield, glass shards splintering through the air, scraping across my face. The saw passes beside me grinding to a halt in the interior of the passenger seat.

The nurse stands there staring at me as I go, I whip the car around and shift into drive. Flying down the bumpy dirt road, I still can't take a breath. I just keep driving. The gates fade away behind me as I go. I make it to the main highway, leading back to town.

I pause in the middle of the road, to make sure I had actually made it out. I inhale as deep as I can, my hands quivering on the steering wheel. No, time to stop any longer, they may still be coming. I shift back into drive and head on down the road.

2:04 A.M.

finally make it back into town, passing by Cory's house, I can't imagine how I am going to be able to tell his family. I keep driving, passing by house after house.

I head through the town till I make it to the police station. I park right up on the front door, and hop out of the car. I limp up to the door and push them open. There is a dispatcher sitting at the front desk, she is wearing a black polo shirt with a sewn-on badge.

I stumble up to the counter and lean on it for balance.

"I need help, my friend has been murdered, there are these crazy people up at the Haddix Asylum. They are experimenting and killing people, they nearly killed me. You have got to send help there!" I plead.

She tilts her head, and squints her eyes at me. She's looking at me as if I'm crazy, she looks down at the counter and presses a button. I let out a breath of exhaustion and stare down at the floor, trying to collect my thoughts.

"Mark? How long have you been having these thoughts? The woman asks.

"What do you mean how long have I...? Wait, did you call me Mark?" I ask confused.

I look back up at the woman, only now she is not wearing a

dispatcher outfit. She is dressed in white, with a small red cross on her hat. Her face is looking at me concerned.

"Yes, that is your name, don't you remember?" She whispers.

I take a step back, I look down at my leg, there is nothing, no cuts, no wounds, I am wearing a white jumpsuit. I look at my side, where I was stabbed, nothing, no blood. I fall to the ground, my breath shallow.

I look around, the room is bright, all painted in white, almost blinding it's so bright. There are doctors pushing patients in wheelchairs going room to room.

A man in a dark suit walks up to me, holding out his hand.

"Mark, are you okay?" The man said.

He looked familiar, his hair was black and greased back, with big framed glasses.

"Mark? It's me Dr. Krane. Can you walk?" He asks.

I give an unsure nod, and he pulls me to my feet. He sits me into a wheelchair and pushes me down the hall.

"Thank you." He says waving to the nurse at the counter.

He takes me through a set of double doors, down a long bright hallway. We go on down the hall till we come up to a room on the left. He points me to the room.

"Here we are." He said.

I glance into the room, it's bright and painted white, there is a small cot in the corner with a small table beside it. Bars cover the window.

"Oh, don't forget your medication." He says handing me a small cup filled with pills.

I stand up and take the cup, I put the cup up to my mouth and swallow its contents. I walk into the small white room and sit on the bed.

"Have a good night Mark, I will be meeting with you again today at seven. See you then." He says shutting the door to the room.

I walk over to the window and stare out, it's a bright sunny day, not a cloud in the sky. I can feel the heat coming in through the windows.

This place looks so familiar, I know I've been here before. I look out towards the front of the building; a small sign is in the courtyard.

Haddix Asylum.

Little Black Hearts

I stood there staring up at the house, cold steel clenched in my right hand. I knew exactly what I had to do. The cool spring breeze is blowing in the air. The sun has disappeared behind the earth. Glints of light shine from the windows as the moon claims the sky.

It's almost time now. Just a bit longer until the last light goes out. That will be when I make my move, that is where this will all end.

One Month Earlier

The final week of winter is finally passed, the snow has left, but a chill remains in the air. I take in a deep breath as I sit on the front steps of my house, watching the farmers drive by in their tractors. The sun is shining, high up in the sky. Everyone on the road passing me by, I'm just a spectator watching life from the outside.

I have never been much of the social type, people never seemed to understand me even when I tried anyway. I typically spend my days alone, just watching the people. I hop up from the steps and begin walking down the sidewalk.

I pass a few old farm houses on my right, a couple of men are dragging hay bales behind the houses. I stare at my feet as I walk, drifting off in my own little world. I hate all of these people, they act like they are all better than me. They call me a freak because I hide in my house all day. They don't know me or what I have going on, who are they to judge, they go through their lives doing the same boring bullshit every day. I watch them, I see what they do. I'd like to burn them all.

They all think they can get away with treating me like shit, thinking that I will stand by and take it, well they are wrong. Everywhere I go they all stop and stare, muttering insults under their breath, thinking I don't hear them but I do. I will show them, make them regret what they have done.

None of them are as bad as the Roberts family, even their children are terrible people. They go out of their way to make sure to tell me what they think of me. Their kids even came to my house and threw eggs at it, the oldest one Jake spray painted freak on my front door. That's okay, I will give them freak, I will make them all pay.

You see, as I hide in my house I'm not just sitting there doing nothing, I'm planning, studying the perfect way to get revenge on them, I've plotted it down to the smallest details. I know exactly what I will do.

As I continue down the side walk, I approach the small convenience store on the corner of Maple. I walk in, the store owner Steve Richards is behind the register giving me dirty looks, like I ruined his day for coming in. I walk into the bathroom in the back of the store, locking the door behind me.

I stare into the mirror, looking at myself, I feel just as disgusted by myself as they all do. My blue eyes are bloodshot from lack of sleep, giant dark circles in bags under them. My black hair covers most of my face, putting a shadow over me. My skin is pale white, I never see much sunlight, I look a bit like a vampire. Long black threads stick out from the holes in my jacket, the thing is ancient, I've had it for at least seven years or so.

I turn the sink on and splash water on my face, letting it drip off me onto the floor. I turn around, pushing the door open, I browse around the store for a minute. I don't really need anything, just want to ruin the dick Richards' day.

He stares daggers at me as I glance around, knocking a few items off the shelf. I grab a lighter and walk up to the register. I set it on the counter in front of him. He keeps staring at me, his shiny bald head glowing from the lights above. He is a filthy pile of shit himself, don't see how he can judge me, the dude is a pedophile. He was caught trying to rape some little girl in the park just a month ago, real sick shit. He even got away with it, he has some relation to the mayor or whatever, so I guess they won't touch him. I could take this sick mother fucker out though.

Large ketchup stains fill his white collared shirt, fat fuck. He is wheezing as he stands there, as if the mere idea of standing is wearing him out, it's disgusting. I don't know which is worse, killing the fat pile of shit for his crimes or letting him waste away slowly, living with himself. Either way he deserves to be gone.

He scans the barcode on the lighter, and I throw some loose change at him.

"Get out, you're not welcome here." He shouts at me.

I give him a crooked smile and flip him off as I leave the store. I head back down the sidewalk towards my house. The Roberts family is all outside staring down the sidewalk at me. Mr. Roberts is on the porch holding a small rifle in his hands, a piece of straw in his mouth, he is wearing a pair of dirty old overalls. Mrs. Roberts is sitting on the front stairs, she has a long flowery dress on, it looks like something from the early 1900's. Jake, and his sister Anne are sitting in a couple lawn chairs out front.

They look like twins, both wearing red flannel shirts and blue jeans. Tony and Blair are the two youngest ones, seven or eight I think. They are both swinging on an old tire swing attached to a huge oak tree around the side of the house. Tony has a ripped blue shirt and blue jeans on, while Blair looks like a mini clone of her mother.

They all stare at me like I'm a piece of nasty garbage floating down the sidewalk, I stare right back at them. They won't intimidate me, I'm not scared, they will get what's coming. Fucking hillbillies.

Their house is two stories tall, towering over the sidewalk with its shadow. A fresh coat of white paint covers it, large pane windows fill the first floor, while smaller circular ones are placed on the top. They have a large farm just behind their house, corn is usually filling the now blank field.

I stare at them waiting for them to start in on me, but I won't back down from their gazes.

"What are you lookin' at boy? Don't you eyeball me." Mr. Roberts said, light glinting off his rotten brown teeth.

I just give him a smile and continue to stare at him.

"Hey Trey, what do you think you're doing walking by my house, you freak?" Jake shouted at me.

I keep on my way, wishing death upon them as I stare.

"Trey is a freak, Trey is a freak." Tony and Blair chant as they spin in a circle holding hands.

Keep up your little games all you want, you will all be dead soon. I continue passed their house towards mine. A hand grabs my shoulder, spinning me around. Jake is there, he pushes me, sending me off balance. I hit the ground hard, he jumps on top of me. Jake is smiling, he punches me in my cheeks a few times. I can feel blood building up in my mouth. I refuse to cry out or beg him to stop, I just hold my stare on him and squeeze out a slight smirk.

He lays into me again smacking me in the head.

"You shouldn't have come around here you little piece of shit." Jake said, as he slammed his fists into me again. "Oh, but don't worry, I'll teach you."

His body is too heavy for me to push him off me, he is twice my size, pinning me down against the concrete. His family cheers him on in the distance, laughing at me. He takes a few more shots at me, another to the face and one in my stomach. All the air in my lungs explode from me on impact, I struggle to hold a straight face. He stands up leaning over me. He gives me a quick kick to my ribs, sending a shockwave through my chest.

"Don't you come back, you hear." He shouts as he spits at me.

He walks away, rejoining his clan in their yard, they laugh and watch me as I crawl back to my feet. I don't let them know my pain, won't give them the satisfaction. I stumble a few steps; the world is blurry from the blows to my head. I distance myself from their house, making my way home. I only live about a block away, making me an easy target for them to reach daily.

I stumble up the small steps to my front door and swing it open. I shut and lock the door behind me, making sure they can't come in after me. About a month ago Jake and his sister Anne followed me home and barged in behind me. They caught me off guard and bruised me up pretty bad. I even ended up having to stay in the hospital for a few days.

They had cracked a few of my ribs on my right side and gashed open my forehead. Had to get about twenty stitches, but it's whatever, nothing I could have done about it.

I stumble over to my old worn down sofa and drop my body into it. I pull a half-crushed pack of cigarettes from my jacket pocket and pull one out. I grab my lighter and ignite the cigarette, inhaling the bitter smoke. I let out a sigh, staring at the ceiling as smoke clouds fill the air. Soon.

3

I t's been nearly three weeks since Jake had attacked me, my body still aches where bruises have darkened my skin. I haven't left my house since, no need. Tonight, that changes, tonight everything changes. I'll wait till the sun sets, then I will make my move, hidden in the shadows. Everyone thinks I'm a freak and that's exactly what they will get.

A smile creeps across my face at the very thought of it. True release, true freedom. The capability to get that which is mine, to watch it all play out in front of me like a movie. The inescapable need to watch my dreams become reality. Tonight, yes, tonight. We will show them.

I begin to giggle uncontrollably, adrenaline fills me with excitement in anticipation. Imagining how it all with play out. It's going to be a masterpiece, all painted in red. Yes, I can almost taste it. Such a sinister thing to desire so strongly, but I love it. I need it.

They think they are so special, untouchable. Like they are Gods and I'm a slave to their will, but I will show them God, show them I can take what they have a rip it from them. Make them burn in the hell they put me in.

Yes, that's it, they will feel pain, and I will bathe in it.

4

stood there staring up at the house, cold steel clenched in my right hand. I knew exactly what I had to do. The cool spring breeze is blowing in the air. The sun has disappeared behind the earth. Glints of light shine from the windows as the moon claims the sky.

It's almost time now. Just a bit longer until the last light goes out. That will be when I make my move, that is where this will all end.

I stare up, the lights light finally is snuffed out, a grim smile crosses me. I begin my ascent up to their front door, my steps silent. I push open the front door slowly, avoiding any creaking sound it may make.

I have studied the house for months now, I know exactly where each one of them is. I decide to take the father first, the biggest threat. I make my way slowly up the tall wooden staircase to the second floor. The house is pitch black and silent.

I creep into a short hallway leading to all the bedrooms. I pass by the first couple rooms, heading for the one at the end of the hall, the parents' room. I stop in the hallway, just outside the door, listening for any sound or movement. They are already sleeping, the faint sound of snoring passes through the door, giving me the green light.

I open the door just enough to slip in. Mr. and Mrs. Roberts are both asleep in the bed. I act quickly so no one wakes. I lift the double-edged knife in my hand up and plunge it into the fathers' windpipe, covering his mouth so he doesn't make a sound. Blood spatters out from his neck, spraying the bed. The blood splashes the mothers' face and makes her twitch.

I can't chance her waking, so she's next. I quickly rush to the other side of the bed and slam my knife into her temple. It slides in smoothly; her eyes shoot open but it's too late. I yank the blade from her and watch as they both go limp. Blood pooling in the bed turning the light blue sheets crimson. I wish I had a camera to fully retain the moment. I stare in awe at my masterpiece as it unfolds in front of me. But, I'm not done yet.

I slip back out into the hallway, passing by Jakes room, I'm saving him for last. I make my way into Tony and Blair's room that they share. They may be children but, they are just as corrupted and evil as the rest, I won't have them grow up to do to others as they have to me.

I take my time with the children, fashioning a noose out of a jump rope on the floor. I tie one end to the ceiling fan, the other awaits their throats. I pull a small roll of duct tape from my pocket, and place it over both of their mouths. I give Tony a quick punch in his nose, feeling the bones shatter under my fist. Blood leaks down his face, dripping on his bed.

I lift him out of the bed and tie the noose around his neck. I drop him letting the rope do its job, he dangles there for a moment. His body shakes and writhes as he is suspended above the ground.

Now time for Blair, evil little bitch in training. I drag her from the bed, her eyes pop open. Fear and panic spread across her face. She should have thought about the consequences of her actions before. I smack her head off the ground, knocking her out. I drag her over to the window, and open it. I toss her body out, watching it fall to the ground below.

I clap my hands together quietly, as if to say a job well done. Then I head back to the hallway. I sneak down to the last room on the left, Anne's room.

I slide in through the door, I walk over to her as she sleeps in the bed. I lean in real close, studying her breaths. A smell of coconut rises from her hair, stinging my nose. I go a different route with her, I want her to suffer. She was old enough to know what she was doing was wrong.

I pull another piece of duct tape out and place it over her mouth. She doesn't even flinch. I pull both of her arms out from under her blankets. I take my knife and drag it across both of her wrists. Blood drains out covering her bed, she springs up in the bed. Trying to scream, but the sound is stopped by the tape. I wave at her and smile as she is claimed by panic.

She tries to jump out of bed but she has already lost too much blood. Her legs immediately give out on her, making her collapse. I stand over her, watching her go. She tries to say something, but her mouth fails her again.

Her head drops down, resting against the wooden floor boards. She goes silent, into oblivion. I feel no remorse, I feel nothing. They have taken away any feeling of sympathy I may have had for them. They asked for this, they pushed me here.

One to go.

5

inally, Jake, the last of them, the only one between me and my peace, my freedom.

I walk casually back into the hallway, I no longer care if he wakes. I want him to see this coming. I kick open the door to his room, it slams hard against the wall. Jake jumps up in his bed, looking around in the darkness as I move through the shadows. He fumbles around trying to turn on the lamp by his bed.

As he pulls the drawstring, light floods the room.

"Surprise!" I shout at him, sending my foot into his face.

He flops out of the bed, crashing onto the floor. I keep on him, stomping my foot into his back. He frantically tries to crawl away to safety. I take my knife and grind it down his spine. Blood spills out onto the floor, his shuttered movements painting the floor like a canvas. My art work coming to fruition, it's beautiful.

His panic and pain fills me with unbearable joy. I can't help but let out a loud laugh as he screams in agony. He crawls to his knees, scraping his way into the hallway. I follow, kicking him in the ribs as he tries to escape. He leans against the walls for support, leaving a large blood trail on them.

He nears the stairway, I then help him along. I kick him in his back sending him rolling down the stairs. I walk down behind him. He rolls across the bottom floor, blood sprayed about. He crawls over to the front door, stumbling around trying to open it. His hands slip around the metal door knob from the blood covering him.

The door gives in to him, flying open, the night air sweeping the room with a chill. He crawls out onto the front porch, begging for mercy. I shall give him none.

I walk over his bloodied body and grab him by his hair, dragging him down his front steps. I place his mouth on the bottom step.

"You should have left me alone, all of you. You fucking assholes thought you could treat people like that and nothing would ever happen. Think again!" I screamed, as I stomped my foot on his head.

His teeth fly out, settling on the concrete below, blood gushed down the concrete path. I stared at him as his body went limp. A feeling of relief washes over me. I walk up the steps and sit down at the top, lighting up a cigarette.

I stare out at the night sky, smoke flying into the air. I can't stay here, not long. It's only a matter of time before the cops show up. I know what to do, how it ends.

I stand up and walk down the sidewalk away from the Roberts house. I walk up to my house and grab a jug of kerosene by my front steps, been saving it for the occasion as a backup plan. I pop the cap off the jug a pour it up the front steps and soak the front door. I trail it all through the house, then toss it on the old sofa.

I spark up a cigarette, taking a deep inhale. I toss the cigarette into the fresh liquid on the ground, flames erupt engulfing the entire house immediately.

Ending this night, this life as it began... In flames.

Those Below
The Pines

1

Another crappy cold winter day. The sun is shining down on us as we drive up the road. Snow is piled high, covering every inch of the earth around us. We are on our way up to Sara's parents' cabin in the mountains.

We figured we would take a few days to get away from the stress of the city down below. Sara is riding shotgun shouting out directions as we go. Her long blonde hair is drawn up in a ponytail with a red ribbon tied around it.

She is a walking stereotype, the usual preppy, cheerleading girly girl type. My best friend Harry is driving, he's rocking a pair of old aviator sunglasses. He's your average guy, short, shaggy brown hair, a cheap grey jacket on. Lately he has been letting his beard grow out, says he's trying out a new look, I think he's just too lazy to bother.

Me, I'm stuck in the backseat with my sister Mandy, Harry kicked me out of the front so he could lay the moves on Sara as he calls it. He's had a thing for her since middle school.

He was new at our school, a big nerd to top it off, Sara was the only person that gave him the time of day. Sara brought him over to my place to hang with everyone, and he just never left. So, that's how we all met, he just kind of fell into the group.

My sister Mandy I was just kind of stuck with, it's not that we are close, more that she just won't go away. She's a major outcast in her class, so she just hangs around with me and my friends. She is really shy, always wearing dark clothes and black make up, people don't really understand her.

Over time Sara got to know her, now they are inseparable. Me, I'm your typical skater punk, never cared much what anyone thought of me, just doing my own thing.

"How close are we?" Mandy asks.

Sara spins around in her chair with a smile.

"Not far, maybe five more minutes." She replied. "You guys are gonna love it, it's huge!"

She turns back forward, pointing at a small dirt road.

"That way, almost there." She states.

We drive up the small dirt path, pine trees are everywhere, the air filled with their scent. The trees seem to make up for the lack of oxygen in the mountains. The forest of trees seems never-ending.

The cabin is now in sight, it's a massive three story cabin, not what I had expected when she said a cabin. I figured we would be staying in some old tiny cabin, you know the kind, the small, basically one room cabins, like you see I the movies.

But no, this place is like a mansion made of logs. Maybe this trip won't be so bad after all.

"Jesus, would you look at that thing." Harry says in awe, lifting his shades as though it may not be real.

We drive up and park in front of the cabin, our car looks like an ant in comparison. We pile out of the car, and stand there all staring at the cabin.

"Told you, you guys would love it." Sara says.

"Damn Sara, how do you guys afford this thing?" Harry asks.

Sara scratches her head for a second looking at the ground.

"Oh! My dad is in some kind of timeshare with this place, I'm pretty sure."

I shake my head chuckling.

"Oh, I see, so your dad fell for one of those bullshit scams eh?" I laugh.

Sara just shrugs her shoulders and bounces up the front stairs to the cabin. Harry and Mandy grab their bags from the trunk of the car. I didn't bother packing anything, figured I wouldn't stick around long enough to need anything.

Harry has a huge bag filled with all sorts of random junk, he thinks he is some kind of survivalist. He is big on dangerous hikes and goes on long camping trips all the time. The thought of camping makes my skin crawl. I live too much in the age of technology, I mean really, why would mankind spend so much time perfecting the indoors just to go stay in the woods and all that, I'll pass.

The area around the cabin is empty, the pine trees are all cut back away from the building, creating a circle around the cabin. There are all sorts of different paths into the woods from hikers, leading into the forests. No doubt Harry will make us go on some stupid hiking trail around here before we leave.

I make my way up the stairs to the cabin. Even the stairs seem unusually fancy for being in the woods, almost like a fake wood, too perfect looking. I walk in through the front door, the place is gigantic, there is a wide staircase in the middle of the room, leading up to the next floor, another staircase from there goes up again.

The lights have a dim glow, they have a cage around the lights made of deer antlers, real hillbilly style. Old paintings of cowboys and horses fill the main sitting area. Several deer heads are mounted in between the paintings. I don't get it, I mean who looks at their walls and thinks, you know what I need? I need a dead deer head stuffed and mounted on the wall, it's ridiculous.

On the other hand, there is a massive flat screen television sitting on the table in front of a long leather couch, now that is more my style.

"I call dibs on the tv!" I shout.

"Really? You came all the way up here to sit and watch tv? Where's the adventure? Where's the excitement?" Harry questions, looking up in the air as if he's already envisioning it.

"What do you mean? If I want adventure, I'll simply watch an action movie, then boom, action, adventure, excitement! I don't even have to move to experience it." I smirk.

"Suit yourself, but I will get you off that couch sometime." Harry states.

I wave him away as I plop onto the couch, it's so soft I sink deep into the cushions, ah, now this is vacation.

2

"**O**h, my God!" Mandy yells. "There is no cell service up here!"

"That's the point." Sara says with a laugh.

Mandy has a look of complete disappointment on her face, she stares, mouth open at Sara.

"How is that the point? What am I supposed to do here now?" Mandy pleads.

Sara giggles at her, then points at the window.

"Um, hello! The whole world is out there, take in some nature, kick back, chill, you know you can make it three days without your phone. I mean look at me, I live on that thing, I'm just fine." Sara said.

Mandy droops her shoulders down, with a sad face.

"But, it's cold outside in nature." Mandy whines.

"Put on a coat then cry baby." Sara says.

Mandy walks away complaining. Sara bounces around, up the stairs.

"Hey Jay? Where did Harry go?" Sara asks me.

I shrug my shoulders.

"I don't know, probably playing soldier outside." I reply.

She turns around, back down the stairs, and out the front door, letting an icy cold breeze in, making me shiver for a moment.

Too damn cold, I don't know how people can live here, if I had the money I'd be gone. I would go somewhere warm year-round, probably like, Florida or Georgia or something, I don't know, anywhere but here.

I flip through a few channels on the tv, nothing but static. Great, there goes my plan. I let out a sigh, and hop off the couch. I guess I'll go see what Mandy is doing. I head up the stairs, they are a deep brown color, they look like they were recently cleaned, still a bleach smell coming from them.

"Mandy! Where you at?" I shout.

"In here!" She shouts from a small room on the second floor.

This floor is laid out in the same fashion as below, more deer heads and paintings fill the walls, candles are mounted for light along the hallway. I go down the hallway toward the small room. She is sitting on a bed too large for the room, messing with her phone.

"Can you believe there is no service up here?" She asks.

"Eh, no surprise, the tv doesn't even work." I respond.

"It's madness!" She says, slamming her phone down on the small table by the bed.

"Tell me about it." I say.

She crosses her arms and frowns, looking up at me.

"So, what are we gonna do now?" She asks.

I shrug rolling my eyes, letting out a sigh.

"Well, I suppose we can see what Mr. Commando, and the fairy are doing." I joke.

She lets out a breath of dissatisfaction and stands up, we head down the hallway, down to the bottom floor.

"I think they went outside." I say.

"Great, out in the cold, just how I wanted to spend my day." She complains.

I zip up my jacket as high as it will go, preparing for the blast of icy air. I open the door and we head outside, the snow crunching under my feet with every step.

"Harry! Sara! Where you guys at?" I shout.

"Over here!" Harry responds.

Damn it! I knew that psycho was going to drag me on some stupid hike. Sara and Harry are standing at the entrance to a trail just behind the cabin, waving us over. He has a sort of hatchet in his hand, the guy is mental.

We walk over to meet them at the trail, the snow getting deeper as I go, trying to pull me down into the ground, swallowing my feet.

"You people are nuts, it's cold as shit out here." I say.

Harry smiles, icicles clinging to his beard already.

"Come on, Sara said there are some cool caves down this trail."

"Great, I love caves, and walking, and cold snow, this is all like living a fairytale." I say sarcastically.

Mandy is clenching her arms, shivering in the cold, her face buried in the top of her coat.

"I hate you all." Mandy claims.

We start down the trail, footprints left in the snow from the last crazy person to brave the winter have matted the snow down, making it easier to walk on. Deer and other small animal tracks are mixed into the footprints. The crushed snow forms a hard, ice like surface, still crunching below our steps.

The sun is bouncing off the snow, making it hard to see. Pine trees are surrounding us on both sides, the air is thin, even with all the trees.

"How far away are these, so-called caves? I'm turning into a popsicle." I ask.

Harry peeks over his shoulder looking back at me.

"Oh, maybe another half mile or so." He says.

Good God, I wish I didn't ask. Mandy is trailing behind, walking slowly, still shivering. She looks miserable, I know the feeling, this sucks. Harry and Sara are walking along as if it's summertime up there.

You can hear birds chirping in the distance as they fly through the sky. Assholes are probably laughing at me as they head south.

We go on and on down the trail, seems like forever.

"What is that?" Mandy asks, pointing into the trees to the left.

Everyone stops and looks.

"What is what?" Harry asks.

She keeps pointing into the trees.

"Over there, I heard something moving." She says.

"Probably a deer or something." Harry said.

We start walking again, Mandy stares into the trees, searching for anything moving as she goes.

"There it is again; don't you hear it?" She pleads.

Harry looks back at her.

"I don't hear anything." He states.

"Something is moving in there, I know it!" She shouts at him.

Harry ignores her and keeps moving forwards, I turn around and walk with Mandy.

"I'm sure it's nothing sis." I say. "Let's just keep going and get this over with."

"Okay, fine, but I know I saw something." She whimpers.

We walk for another few minutes and come up to a small stream, it managed to keep flowing even in this cold. The water is so clear you can see the rocks underneath.

"Over there!" Sara shouts. "That's one of the caves!"

The stream leads directly into the opening of the cave, it must go straight through it. We follow the stream over to the cave, as we get closer the air shifts into a warm, humid breeze. The cave looks like a giant hole in the side of the mountain.

Jagged rocks protrude out around the opening, the snow is all but melted as we approach.

"Dude, this is awesome, we gotta go in and check it out." Harry says.

"No way! I am not going in there!" Mandy interrupts.

"It's pitch black in there, how are we going to see anything?" Sara adds.

Harry drops his bag and starts digging around in it, he pulls out a handful of glow sticks. He stands up and hands a few to each of us.

"There, no problems, now we can see where we're going." He states.

Mandy is terrified of the dark, back home she still spends every night with a light on in her room. I guess she never quite got over that childhood fear.

Mandy walks up and grabs onto my arm, holding onto me for dear life as we walk into the cave. Harry bends his glow stick till it makes a clicking sound, green dim light floods the area from the stick.

The cave is slick with a moss like substance covering the ground, rocks stick out from the walls just waiting to snag you as you pass by them. The stream continues to flow through the cave as far as I can see.

A faint sound of bats shrieking is heard echoing off the walls as we go. Harry throws down a few glow sticks as we walk, so that we can find our way back out. It's so dark in here you can only see about fifteen feet ahead, if not for the glow sticks we would be completely screwed.

"Isn't this beautiful?" Sara said. "How is it so warm in here?"

"I don't know, the cold must not be able to reach the cave." Harry replies.

We keep walking down deeper into the caves, small tunnels are carved through the rocks on both sides of the cave. I wonder where they lead? They seem almost man made. Small pieces of wood go around the tunnels, some kind of bracing system.

"Did this used to be some sort of mine or something?" I ask.

Sara shrugs her shoulders. "I don't know, maybe, if so they haven't used it for as long as I can remember." She says.

"You guys wanna investigate?" Harry whispered.

I really don't want to, but it seems pointless to speak up, Harry will just call me a coward and drag me into it anyway, why bother arguing.

Mandy shakes her head. "No way! You guys can go, I'm staying right here. I've had enough darkness for one day." She stated stomping her foot down.

"Suit yourself, here take a few more glow sticks, these should keep you going till we're back." Harry said, handing her a big pile of glow sticks.

Sara huddles up against Harry as we start into the small tunnel. Why do I let him get me into this crap, I could be back up at the cabin, kicked back and relaxing, but no, I'm in some dark cave tunnel? What the hell?

The tunnel stinks, it's got a thick, damp, musty closet smell coming from it. Kind of a rotten eggs smell to top it off, like sulfur. Tiny hanging lights are spaced out along the wooden braces, they all seem to have been broken or blown out.

This definitely had to be some kind of mine at some point. The ground is moist, making a squishing sound, like walking through a puddle. It seems like the dirt had been disturbed recently, scratch like tracks are scraped through the ground, looks as if someone took a rake to it.

"Do you guys see that?" Harry asked, tossing a glow stick ahead of us. "What is that?"

The glow stick lands a few yards ahead, lighting up what appears to be a small wooden shack, most of the wood is ripped to pieces, leaving chunks of the wall wide open. Looks like something wanted in, or out. Claw like scratches are visible along the small broken door to the shack.

"What could have done this?" I say.

We walk over to the shack, Harry inspects the claw marks, he has a puzzled look on his face. I continue past him into the shack. Small pieces of papers are shredded in the dirt. A splintering table is against the back wall.

Old water damaged papers are laid across the table, one appears to be a picture of a group of people wearing mining gear, it looks ancient, all in black and white.

Another paper on the table reads warning across the top, but you can't make out any of the words on it, too damaged. The last paper looks like some kind of telegraph, none of the words are legible, someone has scribbled through the words.

Harry walks over to me, still looking unsure what could have made those marks.

"You find anything?" He asks.

"No, just some old papers, you?" I reply.

He scratches his beard, staring off at the floor. "No, not really. I have no clue what was down here."

"Hey guys, come here." Sara shouts

She is crouched on the ground outside the shack, holding a small piece of wood.

"Check this out. Some kind of sign, I think." She says.

Harry takes the piece of wood from her, holding it up too his face. It looks like an arrow, don't know where it was pointing anymore, it looks like it was torn out of the ground.

"Does it say anything?" I ask.

Harry squints at the piece of wood. "Well, it's hard to say, it's so old and warped the letters have disappeared. I can see an M and an E then just the number three." He said.

Hmm, that's useless. Harry tosses the sign down, putting his hands on his hips.

"Well, you guys have enough adventure today?" Harry asks.

I nod. "Yeah, I'm good."

Sara huddles back up to Harry and smile at him.

"Alright, let's head back then, almost out of glow sticks anyway." He said.

We start heading back up the tunnel towards the cave entrance, the sound of bats has all but disappeared. The silence is unnerving.

The tunnel seems to be longer going back, maybe it's just me. Small weeds and dead branches stick out from the ground, snagging on my jeans as I walk. A chill has begun to fill the small tunnel, like a gust of wind, making me shiver a bit.

A small clicking sound begins to echo through the tunnel, moving faster and faster, the echo is loud and rhythmic. The sound hits my ears like a ringing, making the hairs on my neck stand up. I feel as if it's getting closer.

The sound is getting even louder it's right on top of me, my heart starts beating faster. The sound is right behind me now, I start running nearly smacking into Harry. Then a loud shrieking sound pierces through me as a swarm of bats flies overhead.

"Holy fuck!" I scream, flailing my hands in the air.

Sara let's out a loud screech as Harry just laughs at us.

"It's just a few bats guys, calm down." He says.

"God damn rats with wings is what they are!" I exclaim.

We reach the exit of the tunnel, Mandy is nowhere in sight. Glow sticks are in a pile on the ground, where we had separated from her.

"Mandy? Where you at?" I shout.

"Mandy?" Sara yells.

No answer, I begin to panic, I run around the area searching for her. Harry runs out of the cave searching, nothing. No sign of her anywhere.

"Where could she be? She wouldn't just leave, it's not like her." I say.

Sara has a terrified look on her face, she's on her knees staring at the ground. She puts her hand to her mouth.

"It's blood!" She whispers.

Harry and I run over to her. Small drops of blood are scattered across the ground. The drops lead to another tunnel across the cave, near the stream.

3

We follow the blood to the tunnel, we pause trying to see anything moving.

"Mandy!" Sara yells into the tunnel.

It echoes on and on bouncing off the walls. Silence.

We start walking down into the tunnel following the trail, the drops of blood are getting bigger. There are marks in the dirt that look like drag marks. Large animal prints are beside them, maybe a bear made them I thought.

"Hold up guys, this stick is out of juice." Harry said.

He reached in his pack and pulled out another glow stick.

"Better find her fast, this is my last one." He stated.

As we go further down the tunnel the smell of sulfur comes back into the air. The blood drops are getting further apart, like it's moving faster.

"Oh, my God!" Sara screams pointing at a small hole in the tunnel wall.

There is a skull with a miner's helmet filling the hole, almost like a decoration, or a warning. The skull is fractured in half, missing its jaw bone, looks like it's been here for a while.

"Keep moving." Harry yells to her.

The tunnel begins to get wider as we go, forming into its own cave.

We come to a large open area, where the stream meets into a small waterfall going up higher into the mountain cave. Another series of tunnels are laid out on all corners of the area.

The blood drops lead us to a small tunnel on the far end near the base of the waterfall. As we approach the tunnel we are sprayed by the crashing falls of the water, soaking us. The water has washed away any blood near the tunnel.

We can hear a crunching sound in the tunnel echoing back to us. It sounds as if someone was chomping down on a bag of potato chips. A few feet into the tunnel, the blood drops reappear. This tunnel is smaller than the last, we have to walk single file through. The air is thin, making it hard to breathe.

I feel claustrophobic as I go, getting light headed. Panic is rising in me the further we go, I can feel a cold sweat pouring out of me. We have to find her.

The blood drops are now becoming small pools on the ground, we must be getting closer. The tunnel begins to widen, coming to another large area, it's so dark in here. The crunching sound has stopped as we walk into the large space.

Harry shines the glow stick around, but the trail has ended.

"Where the hell did it go?" He asks.

He is spinning in a circle searching the ground for anything that could lead us in the right direction.

Sara is frozen in place, staring up above us.

"H... Harry? What is that?" She whispers, as she points in the air.

I look up, there are two glowing white dots, like cat eyes in the night. Harry shines the glow stick up above us.

I can't move. Frozen in shock, my stomach turns on me and I can't keep the bile from shooting out of me.

Sara and Harry stare up at the sight. It's Mandy's body, hanging from a rock formation above the cave. Her head has been ripped from her spine, blood spilling down to the ground, her clothes have been ripped to shreds.

The creature stands on her body claiming its feast as it bites into her back. It glows in the light, a pale white creature, it has piercing white eyes. The creatures head resembles a snake with only slits for nostrils and ears, its teeth are like long ice picks.

It's enormous, long boney arms and legs with claws like razor blades digging into Mandy, ripping her apart.

The creature turns its gaze to us and lets out a shriek, it's so loud I almost collapse from the pain in my ears. I look back up and it's gone.

"We have to move, now!" Harry yelled.

We sprint back to the tunnel, I can barely breathe as I run, still frozen in panic. What was that thing.

We squeeze through the tunnel as it narrows, Harry leading the way, glow stick held high. He reaches the end and waves us out.

"Move, move, move!" He shouts.

Sara and I run past him as he follows.

"Over there!" He shouts, pointing at the tunnel that led us here.

Sara runs into the next tunnel, as I follow behind her. The creature lets out another loud shriek that knocks the air right out of us. We freeze, struck with fear.

Harry is just outside the tunnel, shining his glow stick around in the air above him, looking for the creature.

I turn and watch as he drops, he begins screaming.

"My leg!" He screams.

I look in terror as I see the creature standing above him, it bends over and slashes at him with its claws. Harrys leg flies off into the tunnel sending blood splattering all over. He is paralyzed, laying in the dirt, begging for help. There is nothing I can do.

The creature sinks its claws into his back and drags him away. His screams echo through the cave.

4

"No!" Sara screamed, as we watched Harry being drug off.

Without the glow of Harrys light, we were stuck in complete darkness, I hugged the side of the tunnel and began my way through. Sara held onto my hand as we went.

We moved slowly, feeling the walls for guidance. Harry had stopped screaming, which only meant one thing. I can't think about that now, I have to get out of here.

As we neared the end of the tunnel we could see a dim glow of light shining in.

"Almost there, the exit is just outside the tunnel." I say.

Sara is whimpering, still holding onto me. We run out of the tunnel, Sara sprints off ahead to the cave exit. I run trying to catch up, then she freezes.

The creature drops right in front of her, it puts its face right up in hers. I duck behind a rock sticking out of the wall.

It stares deep in her eyes before letting out another shriek. It stands straight up, it's gotta be ten foot tall. The creatures' ribs are protruding from its skin. Sara starts crying softly and closes her eyes.

The creature grabs her by the shoulder, raising her high up to its level. It places its other hand on her head, it begins squeezing as Sara screams. Her head smashes under the pressure, her body goes limp, blood dripping down from her. The creature tosses her body past me, it lands splashing into the small stream.

I stay silent, letting out small quivered breaths. I can hear the creature sniffing the air. It's hunting me.

The creature stalks the ground, sniffing, searching. I peer out, watching it move, it acts almost dog like as it hunts. I wait, watching as it goes into the tunnel we had gone down earlier.

I crouch down, sneaking out past the tunnel. I'm almost there, just a few yards from the exit. I stumble over a pointed rock sticking out of the ground, cutting my knee on the rocks. I hear a shriek from the tunnel behind me.

I turn my head around for a quick look as the creature pops his head out sniffing the air again. It smells me, it looks right at me, mouth wide open exposing its sharp jagged teeth.

It launches forwards at me, I sprint towards the exit. I run with everything I have left; the creature is right on my heels. I'm so close, I look back the creature is running on all fours, slashing its claws at me.

I make it out of the cave, I'm smacked with the icy wind of winter, the cold tears through my wet clothes. It almost burns it's so cold. I keep running, I can't stop now.

I sprint up the trail towards the cabin, I look over my shoulder, the creature is gone, but I know it's not far behind. I run for what seems like forever, my lungs exploding.

The cold is fierce, like a fire burning to my core. Snow is falling around me, my feet crunching through it as I run. The snow fights me back as I push forward, trying to hold me here forever.

I can see the top of the cabin, almost there. I sprint out off of the trail and circle the cabin to the door, busting through it, finally I can take a breath.

5

slam the door shut behind me, I let out a sigh of relief. I close my eyes and slide down to the ground, leaning against the door. I still can't believe I made it out of there.

Then I hear it, that unmistakable shriek. I open my eyes, there it is, right in front of me standing on the staircase, standing tall. Its eyes wide, staring at me.

Those razor claws spread out to its sides, the creature has almost a smile across its face, like it has won me as a trophy. It starts towards me, only ten feet away.

I close my eyes; my time is up.

Angel of Death

The angel of death is not for I
So, do not touch, I'll tell you why
It'll steal your life before your eye
Yes, touch it once you're sure to die

The statue is cold and black as night
If going by stay in the light
It will rip you apart with all its might

Dragging you down into the deep
It will swallow you from your head to feet

So, stay away I warn you dear
To be afraid to show it fear

You may think it's just a lie
But touch it once you're sure to die

No, the angel of death is not for I
So, stay away and save your life

Printed in the United States
By Bookmasters